A MOUSE IS MIRACLE ENOUGH

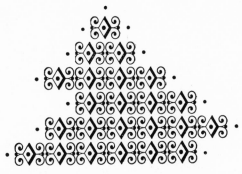

A Mouse is Miracle Enough

MYNA LOCKWOOD

Farrar, Straus & Giroux · *New York*

The author wishes to express
her deep gratitude to Martin Buber
for the inspiration she received
from his book, *I And Thou*.

for a friend, Polly

"But in deede
A friend is never known till a man
have neede."
JOHN HEYWOOD

And a mouse is miracle enough
to stagger sextillions of infidels.

—Song of Myself
WALT WHITMAN

A MOUSE IS MIRACLE ENOUGH

one

In writing of any momentous change in world
events, it is, I think, usually impossible to state with
complete accuracy the time and place where it began
—the turning point. Nor is it always possible to name
the agent that was the prime cause in the change of
events, for a prime cause can assume many shapes.
However, with no guesswork and with complete ex-
actitude I can put my finger on the being that was

the prime cause of a momentous change in the events of my world.

It was a small, humble form of life.

I can also state with accuracy the place of the turning point, and the time when the change in my affairs began. The place was on the East Side of Manhattan, in the Gramercy Park area, where I lived in a studio apartment, which consisted of a bed-sitting room, kitchenette, and bath. The time was late afternoon on the day before a certain Christmas, when the weather was unseasonably warm, with a gray foggy drizzle.

I stood at my huge window of many casements, looking out. The un-Christmaslike weather makes no difference to me, I thought. For aside from Christmas being a religious occasion and a day of obligation to go to Mass, it was like any other day to me. I had hung no holly wreaths in my windows. I would light no candles on the wide sill, to singe my plants. I lived alone, a well-ordered, uncluttered, and sane life, which pleased me and which I intended to keep exactly as it was.

In past times, I had been surrounded by many relatives and by devoted friends who were cultured and important people. But, I mused, I have, with common sense, accepted the fact that as the years pass and a woman moves along toward the inevitable human destination, it is to be expected that, very likely, a husband, relatives, and lifelong friends will get there first, and one by one vanish—*pfft!* I had acquiesced to the plain truth that a lone, aging widow who has no family ties and is living on diminishing capital is not desirable to others as a friend.

"For I can hardly expect new acquaintances to regard me as an asset," I murmured, "but rather as a liability, and I have my pride."

Then I thought of a new acquaintance, Gladys Hall, who like myself was a lone, aging woman. She was an ex-actress, very theatrical and very British, and I didn't much care for her type, but an impulse came to me, from heaven only knows where, to pay a call upon her. I turned from the window and went to put on my outdoor things.

A few moments later, I stepped out of my apartment into the corridor. With my usual care I double-locked my door and closed my screen door, which I'd had put on several summers before, so I could leave my solid door open and thus have cross-ventilation. The screen door was not of the ordinary kind, for the screening was a strong steel, open mesh, of the sort used on some of the animal cages in Central Park. When I was within my home, I had the cozy feeling that the two doors shut out the world, its troubles and inhabitants—that inside I was very safe and snug. Outside, I felt uneasy and exposed—to who knows what?

I felt so now and had a momentary thought of retreating into my domicile. But I set my jaw, took the self-service elevator down, and on Twenty-third Street went into a pastry shop to purchase a fruitcake and have it gift wrapped. Soon I was on a crosstown bus going to the West Side where Gladys lives in a musty renovated brownstone.

Climbing the creaking, dusty stairs, I thought the house, like Gladys, had seen better days. She had confided in me that her husband had deserted her some years earlier, "for fairer and younger fields." Gladys, in an effort to fill the vacancy left in her life, had acquired a parakeet, and named it Armstrong-Jones, but more often she addressed the bird, in excessive affection, by sticky pet names. Really, I thought, she isn't a person I approve of at all, and almost wished I would not find her at home.

But when, out of breath, I reached the top floor, a raucous blast of radio Christmas carols came from the rear apartment. In response to my knock, Gladys threw open the door in her absurd dramatic manner. There she stood: an overage ingénue of the buxom sort. Her large gray eyes were fringed with black artificial lashes, and the corners were elongated by black lines in the currently fashionable Cleopatra makeup. Her hair was dyed red, arranged in a kind of beehive hairdo.

"I say," she exclaimed, "I never thought to see the day when *you'd* come to see me!"

She helped me off with my damp coat, then returned to what she had been doing before my arrival, trimming a little lopsided Christmas tree on her table. The parakeet strutted about the tree, pecking at the strings of popcorn and leaving evidences on the tablecloth that it had not been housebroken.

"Not very hygienic," I said, making a distasteful face.

"Oh, I say! Where's your Christmas spirit?" Gladys shouted above the blare of carols from the radio. Then to the bird, "We don't think cleanliness is next to godliness, do we Tweety-Sweety?" And complacently to me, "I know my bird and my bird knows me." She sent me an amused, friendly glance. "If you can't stand all this merry, merry, darling, turn off the radio."

Even after I had turned it off, Gladys still spoke in clarion tones intended to reach the top gallery of any theatre. "If you aren't doing anything special tomorrow, love, come and have a jolly Christmas dinner with Armstrong-Jones and me. We're having the English traditional—roast beef and plum pudding."

My glance dropped to the bird on the table, and my stomach, which is easily upset, turned queasy. I said, with stiff courtesy, "No, thank you. Christmas is a home day, and I prefer to spend mine there."

"So do I—now that I have Armstrong-Jones to share it with me, bless his little commoner heart." Dramatically she blew a kiss to the bird, and in disapproval I thought, Must she be the actress, morning, noon, and night? And does she think her dyed red hair and garish makeup help her to look younger?

I pressed my lips together in an astringent line. *I* would never resort to such futile efforts to conceal my own aging. No indeed! Yet I didn't let myself go, either. I used eyebrow pencil discreetly. My graying hair was well-coifed. I disciplined the natural appetite of older people for carbohydrates and kept my figure within bounds. And certainly I never, never would think of encasing myself in a getup like Gladys's. My glance went over what she was wearing, a tight black jersey shift, knee-length, exposing her thick, walking-type legs.

"Must you look down your aristocratic nose, darling, at my display of good, solid British legs?" she asked with good humor. And I thought, How carelessly theatrical women use endearments—so that they mean nothing at all.

"Well, love," she said, "if you won't come to Christmas dinner with Armstrong-Jones and me, we'll give you your gift now. Come along, Tweety, darling." The parakeet flew up, lit on her high hairdo, and out they went, returning shortly with a small gift-wrapped box, which Gladys handed to me, and I gave her the larger one I had brought.

"Mine's a fruitcake," I said, and she replied, in her vibrating voice, "Mine's perfume. It's from Sweety-Tweety and me. We hope you like it, darling."

Soon thereafter I departed, thinking derisively, She is strictly for the birds. (My radio kept me abreast of the current colloquialisms.) Imagine being such a fool about a parakeet!

It was blue twilight when, dampened by the misty weather, I arrived at the apartment house where I live. Under the awning, I encountered a bowing acquaintance, a middle-aged bachelor, Mr. Gardiner, who was emerging to walk his dog. He was a lean, stooped man who was always chewing on an uptilted toothpick. His features were drawn and sallow, for he "suffered with ulcers," as I'd overheard him confide more than once to anybody who would listen. Now he seemed unusually cheery as his small brown mongrel pulled him, willy-nilly, across the sidewalk to a sign that read, "CURB YOUR DOG."

"Trudy knows what the sign says," Mr. Gardiner boasted fondly. "Oh, she's a smart little dog, I can tell you."

I noted with disdain that he had tied holly sprigs to the dog's collar with a red bow; from its ribbon ends dangled little silver bells. As the dog jumped about, bells jingling, Mr. Gardiner cackled with delight, his Adam's apple bobbing up and down in his scrawny yellowed neck.

"Hey! Just look! She's as excited as any other youngster on Christmas Eve," he cried, and his nasal laugh hurt my ears. "Her feminine intuition tells her we're going to have a good old-fashioned white Christmas—an out-and-out snowstorm."

"It looks more like rain to me," I observed trenchantly, and continued on my way. How silly can one get about a dog, I thought as I went into the lobby, where the building superintendent was putting up a big and impersonal Christmas tree.

I had to squeeze sidewise into the self-service elevator, for it was crowded with last-minute Christmas shoppers. A small, plump woman had her arms overflowing with evergreens, a heavy bag of something marked "Kleen-Cat," and brown paper sacks from which protruded a chicken's legs, two bottles of sherry, a bottle of whiskey, and a child's red mesh Christmas stocking that bulged with toys.

"It's for Santa Claus to bring to my cat," she explained when she caught me eying it. "I've filled it with things my cat likes. You know—a ball, catnip, and a rubber mouse that can be wound up to run." She laughed and the others joined in. I smiled thinly, but politely I pressed her floor button for her.

She was another bowing acquaintance, one whom I had mentally dubbed the Character with the Cat. I knew she was an old maid who lived on the floor below me, but I did not know her name and didn't want to. Not only was I choosy about people and determined to keep my independence, but I maintained a strict barrier against any possible infringement on my privacy. I did not intend to have gossipy females with time on their hands dropping in on me at all hours, to borrow something and perhaps to pry as to what I lived on—an income, an annuity, or old greenbacks hoarded in tin cans. So I had been deliberately standoffish with the tenants in our building during the many years I had lived in Gramercy Park.

Now this small, pulpy-looking woman spoke to me with some diffidence. "My cat is such good company," she said, in a purring tone. "I'm so grateful to have him to share my Christmas with. Goodness knows, I'm willing enough to share what I have, but on Social Security it surely is a strain to feed a big tomcat." I nodded, and agreed with cold courtesy that, yes, we would have a white Christmas, though inwardly I was certain we would have rain.

When she got off the elevator on her ninth floor, I noted that she was so short she could walk under my outstretched arm as I pressed the button for my floor, the tenth. I raised my eyebrows superciliously at her back view, with its protruding side loads. What a fool to act as a pack donkey and play Santa Claus for a cat!

Shortly thereafter I entered my apartment. With care I hooked my screen door, and as my solid door shut behind me and the lock clicked, I let out a deep sigh of relief. Now the world and its idiotic people were shut out. I switched on the lights, and as a warm yellow glow blessed my neat, snug home I thought, What a comfort to be alone again with my books, my plants and my memories. Thank heaven I had more sense than to clutter up the place with evergreens and holly that would shed needles and red berries on my blue carpeting.

With my habitual care I hung up my damp black cloth coat and put my hat into a hatbox, congratulating myself because I was not one of those imbeciles who try to fill their empty lives with pets. " 'I have learned to be self-sufficing in whatever circumstances I am,' " I murmured in complacence, quoting St. Paul. Not only could I live alone, but I valued my privacy and appreciated the privilege of living my life to suit myself.

I went to open the double doors of my kitchenette. Then, as I lit the gas under a pot of leftover coffee, it struck me forcibly, how alone I was in the world. When one enters into the upper age brackets, I mused, one surely enters into dangerous territory, where cancer and senility can fasten upon one to nibble life slowly away, or strokes and angina pectoris pounce out from ambush to snatch us into kingdom come.

While I waited for the coffee to heat, I ruminated over the sad fact that such slow nibblers and sudden pouncers had decimated my friends and relatives; indeed, at times I felt like a forgotten old dress left on a hanger in the dusty closet of an abandoned house. My one surviving lifelong friend was beset by a slow nibbler and was therefore immobile. At rare intervals she phoned me, but it was not unusual for weeks to pass when nobody did—either phone or visit me. So now and then I suffered from a nagging fear that I might die in the night and no one would know it until—as Martha had said in the Bible of her brother Lazarus—"by this time he is already decayed."

"But if I'm not found until then," I thought in sardonic humor, "it won't be *my* problem."

I carried a cup and saucer to the low coffee table beside my Boston rocker. Then I fetched the steaming coffeepot, placed it carefully on a mosaic tile to protect the table, and, sitting down, slipped off my shoes to ease my tired feet. As I poured the coffee, I reflected that I had not encouraged new people to move into my empty life, because a slow nibbler might fasten upon me and I might linger on and on and on, with my tail feathers dragging, to last longer than my money did.

"In all fairness," I murmured, "I cannot expect new acquaintances to face my problems." And stoically I acknowledged the fact that living alone into old age required fortitude. "Youth could never take it," I muttered grimly.

I sipped coffee and rocked meditatively. But, thank my stars, I had no need of a pet to solace me. Aside from a brief period years before, when I had joined a riding club and formed an aloof acquaintance with a horse, I had never, during my entire life, wanted an animal—not during my childhood, my teen-age, or my childless marriage. So most emphatically in my aging widowhood I did not want one underfoot. "Thank heaven I have no need of a messy bird, a dog to walk, or a cat to feed," I congratulated myself.

Then a peremptory knock sounded at my doors.

Annoyed, I set down my coffee cup. Now who on earth could that be? I called out, "Yes?"

"It's us—Jane and Peter Weatherby."

What brings these children here? I thought in irritation as I put on my shoes. I knew their parents only slightly. They lived on Long Island, and at Thanksgiving time they had searched in their minds, as people do, for a lone soul to invite to their festive and indigestible dinner—and had picked me.

As I went to the door, a premonition nudged me, a foreboding of some calamity. But no, I thought, what is there to be afraid of? Yet when I opened my solid door, and through the screen door saw burgeoning Jane, age eleven, and thin Peter, age nine, standing outside, my apprehensive eyes went straight to a large, square package they carried between them.

"It's a Christmas present for you, Mrs. Wood, so

you won't be lonesome any more," Jane said happily, and Peter, grinning, cried joyously, "Oh boy! Just you wait till you see what it is! Let us in."

With reluctance I unhooked my screen door. They came in and set down their package. Peter cried eagerly, "Shall we open it up for you, Mrs. Wood?"

Trepidation gripped my stomach, but I nodded.

They unwrapped and unwrapped, to the accompaniment of a jingle-jangle, finally revealing a cage in which there was a wheel, with tiny tin bells tied to its spokes. A ridiculous little Christmas tree stood on the cage roof, and to its four corners were tied sprigs of holly. On the cage gate was affixed a miniature white porcelain angel, holding aloft a scroll on which were the words, childishly illuminated in red and green, "BEHOLD! I BRING YOU GOOD TIDINGS OF GREAT JOY."

An overstatement if there ever was one. A long, slow, cold shudder passed all through me as, with the greatest repugnance, I eyed the cage's occupant.

For it was a black mouse.

My inner consternation was indescribable, but outwardly I must have shown a decent spirit of gratitude, because the children seemed satisfied. "We just knew you'd love a mouse," Peter declared, and Jane added, "We saw you watching ours on Thanksgiving Day." And now I regretted that, out of politeness, I had pretended to be amused by their rodent's senseless antics.

Peter gave me some sketchy instructions on the care of a mouse; then Jane said they'd better go because their parents were double-parked on Twenty-second Street.

And they departed.

Left alone with my gift, I stared down with aversion at the small rodent, for I am a throwback to the Victorian females who screamed, lifted their skirts, and jumped up onto chairs when a mouse scooted across the floor. I eyed this one. Again I shuddered. "I'll dispose of the loathsome little beast at once," I said. Perhaps I could steal unobserved down into the basement and turn it loose or—

I remembered the small old maid who lived on the floor below, the Character with the Cat. In my mind rose a clear image of her in the elevator that afternoon, her plump arms overflowing with holiday greens, sacks of groceries, and a red mesh Christmas stocking filled with, among other things, a rubber mouse that could be wound up to run.

I looked speculatively at the rodent.

Well, why not? Surely a real mouse, already wound up to run and be caught, warm and juicy, would be more acceptable. The woman had said that it was hard to feed a big cat on Social Security. The mouse would provide a free meal, a Christmas dinner. And after all, it was only a mouse.

I was on my way to the door when a thought stayed me. I ought to keep the mouse for a few days in case Jane and Peter came in to see how it fared. But saints in heaven, how was I to endure its presence for even a short time?

I scowled down at the rodent, biting my lips. In

anticipation I went over in my mind all the disagreeable things that confronted me: the foul odor that would permeate my small apartment, the daily scrubbing out of the cage to keep it hygienic, the regular feeding of the odious little beast.

"Well, at least, feeding a mouse will not strain my small budget," I murmured sourly. "And I won't have to put it on a leash and walk it to a sign that says, 'CURB YOUR MOUSE.' "

But these advantages did not comfort me. Making a grimace of distaste, I gingerly picked up the cage, and, holding it at arm's length, I carried it into the bathroom, set it down in the tub, where any contamination could be washed down the drain, then hurriedly opened wide the window.

But as I was making a hasty exit, I was suddenly brought to an abrupt standstill by the tinkling of the little tin bells. I returned to the tub. The black mouse was running determinedly on its wheel, as if over hill, over dale, to some distant destination that would take all night to reach. "Now, how am I to get any sleep with that infernal tinkling going on?" I said aloud angrily. Certainly I would not put my hands into the cage to remove the bells; the very thought of it sent cold shivers up my spine. I went out, slamming the door behind me.

Outside the door I stood irresolute. Already it was past my usual dinner hour. The arrival of the nasty little creature had upset my routine. Also my stomach. The very thought of preparing food with a mouse in the apartment made me ill. I'd skip my dinner and go to bed.

As I disrobed in my dressing alcove, I could hear, from beyond the closed bathroom door, the sound of little bells ringing faintly, as if coming from far, far off, through the distance of many years, from long-gone and happier Christmases. And through my mind drifted nostalgic memories of pleasanter yuletide gifts —a bracelet with diamonds, a coat of softest fur, a motorcar.

"And now a mouse!" I exclaimed wrathfully. I felt outraged. "A mouse! So I need not be lonesome any more."

As if living alone need necessarily be lonely. I banged my shoes onto the floor. I had my religion, a sane amount of it, enough to meet the requirements of my church. I went to Mass and Communion every Sunday, and to confession each Saturday evening, less in penitence than because it was someplace to go and Father Lane was somebody sympathetic to talk to— though I was hard put to think up sins to confess.

"For let's face it," I grumbled as I put my long-sleeved flannel nightgown over my head, "I no longer have pleasant opportunities to commit any."

Yet my life was far from empty. For one reason, my days were pleasantly occupied in writing my memoirs. But when I had mentioned this rewarding activity to Father Lane, he had raised his bushy, sandy, nonconformist eyebrows and said in reproach, "Looking back over your shoulder at past events in your life, listening to the ghostly echoes of long-silenced voices—do you call this living?" And this had offended me.

Then he had climbed up onto his high sacerdotal horse and said sternly, "As your spiritual advisor, I direct you to read a certain book. Here, I'll write down the title and the author." I had expected the author to be some erudite Catholic priest, and the book's title to be something like, *Spiritual Exercises in Meditation and Prayer,* but it wasn't.

Now I glanced at the paperback that lay on my writing table (which doubles for dining). The book's author was Martin Buber, its title *I and Thou.* It was a philosophical treatise on "being" and "relation," and hard going for me, for I am no top-drawer intellectual. Usually I read it after retiring, to put me to sleep, but tonight I was in no frame of mind to read philosophy, even as a soporific.

I brought out a carpet sweeper to gather up the needles that had dropped from the miniature Christmas tree on the cage. I bent my arthritic back to pick up red holly berries. Then, as I removed the day cover from my studio couch, I thought how drastically my life had changed. My much prized and guarded privacy had finally been invaded, and by a repulsive little rodent. "So I need not be lonely any more," I repeated. "As if the void in any widow's life could be filled by a mouse!"

Grumbling, I crossed the room to the huge studio window and threw wide its casements. Though the foggy drizzle would stiffen my joints, the plants on the sill would be in no danger of freezing on this warm

Christmas Eve and I would not be asphyxiated by mouse stench.

Then I got into bed, and a miasma of sleeplessness. I tossed. I turned. Faintly I could hear the little tin bells ringing on the wheel as the mouse determinedly, confidently ran on and on and on toward some fancied destination.

"A mouse!" I repeated wrathfully, thumping my pillows. "In this nuclear age, when mankind is concerned with such prodigious projects as jet-propelled capsules orbiting the earth, rocket ships zooming to the moon, and hydrogen bombs capable of destroying civilization, I am expected to concern myself with a mouse."

But as, worn out with fuming, I drifted off into uneasy sleep, I had the direful feeling that a weighty and intolerable responsibility had been put upon me.

two

Christmas morning I woke with a sense of doom. What was it that weighed me down? Then I remembered.

It was a mouse.

Sighing, I got up. I always feel awful in the morning. In my lavender satin mules, I flapped to the casement windows. As I pulled them shut, one after another, I saw that outside there was still a miserable gray drizzle and not the white Christmas Mr. Gardiner's mongrel had supposedly foretold. Then, stoically, I went into the bathroom to face up to my disagreeable gift of black rodent.

Down in the white bathtub stood the cage. The silly mouse-sized Christmas tree was askew on its roof; the holly sprigs on its four corners and the porcelain angel on its gate were shaking violently as the mouse ran pell-mell on its wheel. "Getting nowhere very fast," I said contemptuously. But it crossed my reluctant mind that it was not unpleasant to hear the merry tinkle of little bells, to see some signs of yuletide decorations and a living creature manifesting joy on Christmas morning.

However, the strong odor of mouse was disagreeable—very. Making a face, I hastily retreated into the living room.

It was my usual custom to do my hair and put on a fairer face and my lavender housecoat before I breakfasted. Instead, on this morning I remained in my hair rollers and flannel nightgown as I flapped about in my mules working out a hygienic method of taking care of the mouse—not for its comfort, but for my own. Preparatory to scrubbing the cage and feeding the obnoxious little creature, I carefully spread newspapers over my writing table, and then brought out a jar of sunflower seeds and a small wire box, gifts that had accompanied the mouse.

Next, very gingerly, and again at arm's length, I fetched the cage to the table and placed the wire-mesh box close to it, with the apertures vis-à-vis. Then, holding my nose and looking the other way, I waited for the mouse to go from one into the other.

When I looked, it hadn't. It wouldn't.

I remembered that when Peter had told me how to take care of the rodent, he had said that one must never grab a mouse by its body (repulsive thought), for one might inadvertently crush its tiny ribs. "The way to handle a mouse," Peter had said, "is to swing it by its tail." I shuddered. Never, never would I so much as touch a mouse, let alone swing it by its slimy, almost prehensile tail.

I sat down to wait for the obstinate little beast to go from the cage into the box. I noted that it was a rather thickset rodent—possibly a peasant type—for Jane had said it was a field mouse. "And peasants are prone to be dull-witted and slow to act," I murmured. Or perhaps it was middle-aged and had a middle-aged spread. Undeniably it was a lone mouse on Christmas Day—perhaps a widow—

"Oh, for crying out loud!" In exasperation, I got up quickly. "I can't wait all day on that stupid, disgusting slowpoke of a little beast." My head was splitting because I hadn't yet had my coffee. I snatched up the wire box and cage, angrily shook the mouse from one into the other, and hooked down the box lid. Then, again holding the smelly cage at arm's length, I took it to the bathtub, which I had previously filled to the brim with hot, sudsy water, and dropped the cage in—Christmas decorations and all.

The cage sank. Spitefully I wished the mouse was still in it. The splash had caused the tiny Christmas tree and holly sprigs to come loose. They floated, together with the soaked scroll, its childishly printed red and green letters smearing together. But the porcelain angel promptly sank—and my heart with it. "Oh, my Lord! I can't let an angel drown," I said. I dropped stiffly to my knees, plunged a hand in, soaking my sleeve to the elbow, and fished up the angel.

The little bells tinkled as later I scrubbed the cage vigorously, using all my resentment and available disinfectants, antiseptics, and deodorants. My resentment grew into anger that veered against the children's mother. There is no excuse for her, I thought. She knows that mice are welcome pets for kindergarten children. The very idea! Letting Jane and Peter give me—a mature woman—a mouse for Christmas!

I got madder and madder.

As I carried the clean cage back into the living room, the realization struck me forcibly that soon it would be messy and smelling to high heaven again. "So why put the horrid little animal back into it?" I questioned aloud. And my previous idea for getting rid of the mouse returned temptingly. It would make a fine Christmas dinner for the pulpy little woman's cat.

But the condemned are always given a good meal before execution, I thought. I dumped a generous amount of sunflower seeds into the wire box. "There! Eat your fill before you die," I said. The small tubby rodent inspected the seeds with deliberation, discarding one after another. "For what reason, for heaven's sake?" I asked. I could not tell one seed from another; they all looked exactly alike to me. Finally, the mouse chose one, sat up on its haunches, and munched contentedly. After a full meal of carefully selected seeds, it washed its face and paws with fastidious thoroughness. "Why, it has hygienic notions—like me," I murmured.

Then I remembered that I had to keep the mouse a few days just out of politeness to the children. So, warily, I shook the rodent out of the wire box and back into the spic-and-span cage. I took it to the studio window, which has a wide sill where I keep green growing things—philodendrons, snake plants, Chinese lily pads in a square glass bowl—such hardy growths as require no sun and are little bother. Midway on the sill I placed the metal cage.

Next I cogitated. The children had told me that mice were nocturnal creatures and usually hid all day to sleep. This one had no place to hide in. So I cut newspapers into shreds, while a dismal gray rain slushed against the windowpanes. What dreary Christmas weather! I thrust the shredded paper into the bare cage, saying, "There! It can hide its loathsome self and sleep." But it wouldn't.

The little bells chimed as it climbed onto the wheel and took a last fling. As if just being alive, even in a cage—as if just having legs to run on, even getting nowhere—was such a wonderful experience that it couldn't bear to take time out to sleep. At my own bedtime, I was only too glad to crawl into sleep and forgetfulness. Sighing, I turned away.

My usual morning custom was to take a hot bath to limber up my arthritic joints, but now the very thought of getting into the tub where I had scrubbed a mouse cage turned my stomach, so I took a shower. I dressed, did my hair, and returned to the living room, and saw no mouse. Thanks be, it had hidden at last. I could forget it and have my breakfast. I glanced at the clock—oh, no, I couldn't. Where had the morning gone? I'd have to forgo breakfast or Communion.

With my head still aching, and casting vindictive glances at the mouse's cage, I put on my coat, hat, and galoshes, grabbed my missal and umbrella, and set out for Christmas High Mass.

Now, on ordinary days I take the short walk to my parish church in Gramercy Park, but on such special occasions as Christmas, Easter, and confessions, I have my good reasons for taking a long bus ride up to Eighty-fourth Street to go to a Jesuit church on Park Avenue, although I heartily dislike its enormousness, its ostentatious architecture, and its interior mishmash of Byzantine with heaven only knows what else. I especially dislike its fashionable congregation and the roped-off pews. But I do like its choir music, which is one of the good reasons I go there.

That Christmas Day, as the choirboys came in procession down the center aisle singing jubilantly, "Angels we have heard on high, sweetly singing o'er our plains," I, too, felt an upsurge of spirit. Then I remembered the white porcelain angel on the cage, and what the cage had brought to me, and my momentary joy curdled. The choirboys, passing the pew where I sat, were singing, "While our hearts in love we raise, Gloria in excelsis," but my own heart sank to a new low.

At the finish of Mass, my plain black cloth coat exited among the many expensive coats of high-toned animals—sables, minks, and silver foxes. When I came out into the lobby, I saw, near the ornate marble font of holy water, the other good reason why I take the long bus ride up to Eighty-fourth Street, Father Lane.

Though it is not customary at this church for any of the many priests to stand in the drafty lobby and speak to parishioners at the close of Mass, Father Lane was doing so. His black cassock and his thinning hair blew in the wind, his bright blue eyes twinkled beneath his unruly sandy brows, as he said heartily to one and all, "Merry Christmas, and may the Christ Child bless you!" And to a favored few, whose circumstances and foibles he knew, he added something personal.

As I tarried, waiting for his glance to fall on me, I reflected that of late he had shown unusual concern about my circumstances and foibles. On one occasion, he had said lightly, "Living alone and liking it can stem from selfishness." Once, more seriously, "Severing relations with the world can cause one to become ingrown—even queer—a *character*." And recently, jokingly, "The first thing you know, you'll be talking to yourself."

But now he saw me, and wished me a Merry Christmas as if he really cared. Then he asked anxiously,

"And how are you spending your Christmas, Mrs. Wood?"

"I am *not* spending it alone," I replied loftily. Then, as his good red-cheeked face lit up, I added lugubriously, "I am spending it with a mouse," and left him looking startled and uneasy as I raised my umbrella among the others and went down the rain-wet stone steps.

The moment I entered my apartment, my glance went to the window sill and the cage. The mouse had emerged to snoop about. Maybe it was thirsty. I put water in a bottle cap and offered it. The mouse sniffed it and turned away. I had known men who scorned water—but a mouse? I was puzzled. It leaped upon the wheel to run swiftly. "Why, for heaven's sake?" I asked.

I removed my wet coat and galoshes, opened my umbrella and put it in the tub to dry, and returned to the living room. The rodent still ran and ran, and the whirling wheel made me dizzy, for my head had settled down to a hard, steady throbbing. But at last I could have my coffee.

As I went toward the kitchenette, the phone rang. It was Gladys. "Won't you change your mind and come to three-o'clock dinner with Armstrong-Jones and me?" she asked in her strident voice.

It occurred to me that she was lonely, even with her bird. I had a momentary wild impulse to go with my mouse—not in sympathy, but just to see her expression when she admitted us. She didn't mind bird dirt, so she wouldn't mind mouse dirt. She would think the four of us "just jolly." But I felt my mouth draw into a sour line. No, I would not be another such fool.

"I'm just about to have my breakfast, and it's noon," I told her, and added, "I'm sorry but I should have no appetite at three o'clock—especially for a Christmas dinner."

After I hung up and turned again toward my kitchenette, I saw that outside the huge window a few snowflakes were now mixed with the rain. On the sill, the mouse had hidden to sleep again. "Thank goodness," I said fervently. Now I could have my coffee and forget that I was spending Christmas with a mouse.

The rodent remained invisible all the long afternoon while I struggled with Martin Buber's *I And Thou,* trying to make some sense out of it. When I read, "At times the man, shuddering at the alienation between the *I* and the world, comes to reflect that something is to be done," I thought, It's Father Lane who reflects that something is to be done about *my* alienation. Then I sniffed. My alienation was permeated by strong mouse odor. I laid down my book with a groan.

"Oh, no! Not again!" I protested. I thought of repeating the transfer of rodent from cage to box, of removing the shredded paper, now interspersed with mouse droppings, of filling the bathtub with soapy water, of scrubbing the cage. "Never!" I cried aloud. I sprang to my feet. "I will not go through all that again. I'll get rid of that unhygienic little beast at once."

With determination, I went out into the corridor. Though I did not know the name of the Character with the Cat, I knew she lived in 9-A. Not waiting for the elevator, I ran down the flight of stairs and rang her bell imperiously. When she opened the door, she looked astonished to see that it was I.

Hastily I explained. "Some well-meaning children gave me a Christmas present of—er—a pet—"

"Oh, how sweet," she interrupted, in a soft breathless voice. "What a sweet gift! A pet! What is it? Do come in and have a glass of Christmas sherry."

"I really can't, thank you," I replied stiffly. "I have only a moment. It is—er—a pet your cat is sure to like."

"Oh, how sweet," she said again, in her eager, purring voice, and I thought, She has a limited vocabulary, as is usual with people of no cultural background and family. "I bet I can guess what you've come for," she was saying. "No, don't tell me—I'm as intuitive as an animal. They are, you know. You have come to borrow some of my Kleen-Cat deodorant sand. Now, do come in. I'll gladly let you have a jar full." ⦁

Reluctantly I entered. "Go right into the living room," she urged, flurried but hospitable, "and present yourself to my cat, Cassius, while I get the sand."

I had to edge into the room sidewise because the furniture was so crowded together that the place re⦁

sembled a storage warehouse. It was a room of deep shadows, the daylight obscured by red plush drapes. As my eyes grew accustomed to the gloom, I glimpsed a Savery highboy, an ebony piano inlaid with mother-of-pearl, a marble-topped bureau, a grandfather clock, a Bible box, a banjo clock. On the walls hung wool-work mottoes and steel engravings, one of weeping willows drooping over a gravestone in the rain. Finally, between a French Renaissance chest and a huge Russian malachite vase, I located her cat.

On a folded rug it lay—a long, gaunt orange-colored feline stretched out asleep alongside the red Christmas stocking, now empty. The rubber mouse lay between the cat's front paws. He felt my gaze, woke, and stood up stretching—a lean, caved-in-looking cat. I murmured, " 'Yond Cassius has a lean and hungry look.' "

"And 'Would he were fatter,' I say with Julius Caesar," said the little woman ruefully. I was startled by her noiseless entrance, as if on paws, and surprised because she had quoted Shakespeare. She shoved aside a Sèvres vase and some supermarket magazines on a piecrust table to make room for a glass jar of sand.

"There! This will solve your problem. Now we must have that drink of Christmas cheer." Silently she padded out in her furred, oversized house slippers, and returned with a crystal decanter and two glasses. As she poured, my critical eyes took in her short frowzy burnt-orange hair, her pudgy round face, with its transparent skin and dimpled chin, and the curves of her small body which overstrained the capacity of her wrinkled mauve-colored dress.

"Taking an inventory of me?" she said, looking directly at me with small eyes as green as June crab apples. "I took off my girdle after Cassius and I ate our fill of Christmas dinner. My cat and I both love comfort. I dyed my hair to match my cat. Silly, aren't I?" Smiling, she handed me a glass of sherry.

"Isn't this room a holy mess? But I can't afford to pay storage charges. I suppose I ought to dispose of all these family heirlooms—I'm the last survivor of the line—but Grandmother put the obligation to protect them on me. You should have known Grandmother. She hid her blushes behind a lace fan at the mention of a chicken's breast. Anyway, I'm the captive of old furniture and—" Her soft voice trailed off.

Then she lifted her glass, saying briskly, "Well, here's to a Merry Christmas and a Happy New Year. Now, let's sit down, drink a toast to our cats, and get acquainted."

"I'm sorry, but I cannot stay." Standing, I took three polite sips of my sherry. She tossed hers down her throat as I had seen tough laborers drink. Uneasily I set down my half-emptied glass. "I really must return to my own domicile, as I have urgent duties to attend to." I was aware that I spoke pedantically. Was it because I so rarely conversed with people? In my solitude, I was easy enough in the mental conversations I carried on—even slangy.

"Well, if you must go," she began in a plaintive tone, adding quickly, "You won't mind if I have another glass before you leave, I'm so tired of drinking alone." After she had tossed off another, she cried in tipsy gaiety, " 'Heigh ho, the holly. Life is most jolly,'

I sing with Shakespeare." Then she said with concern, "I've just thought of something else you may need—milk. I'll be glad to lend you some for your cat."

"I need no milk, thank you," I replied, edging out between the fine old furniture toward the door. The orange cat rubbed against my ankles, purring, and his mistress followed me on her own soft paws. As she opened the outer door, she inquired, "Is yours a female? No, don't tell me. I have a hypersensitivity toward people—I can read their minds. Well, my intuition tells me now that your pet is a female, and we can mate her to my Cassius and get some sweet little kittens."

"No, we can't," I said shortly, and left the tomcat looking snubbed in his virility, and the frowzy woman wide-eyed and her face quivering. Looking as if she were fatally wounded and bleeding to death internally, I thought. Such sensitivity was a weakness, and if there was one thing I abhorred, it was weak women. I had no patience with them.

Feeling that a weak woman had thwarted my purpose, I stamped up the stairs. What a character! I thought. She and her intuition. It had been as far off as the mongrel dog's supposed intuition about the weather. I was vastly irritated at the woman's inaccurate conclusions. But why hadn't I told her she was wrong on all counts—except possibly sex, for I had no idea whether the rodent was a she or a he. To me it was an 'it.' And why hadn't I told her what species of animal it was—and that I had called not to borrow for it but to donate it to her cat?

"I should have taken the infernal mouse down with me—not gone down first to ask if it was acceptable," I told myself as I opened my screen door and unlocked my solid door.

As I entered, the odious smell of mouse met me head on, and I thought bitterly that Providence seemed more intent upon saving the life of the mouse than my own, for its odor surely would be the death of me. "Well," I said dryly, "let's hope this Kleen-Cat stuff will do the trick even if this 'it' isn't a cat." Then I opened the casement windows wide, to let in fresh air—and, incidentally, some snow—and took the cage into the bathroom.

As soon as I had emptied it of mouse, I removed the tiny bells from the wheel. "Here we go again," I said, in a martyr's tone, and proceeded to scrub the cage. When it was immaculate and its floor covered with the deodorant sand, I shook the black mouse back into it and returned cage and mouse to the window sill, closing the casements and sending the snow flying. Then I supplied a supper of sunflower seeds, and, thinking of milk, filled a bottle cap full. The mouse lapped it up thirstily, and I murmured, "Well! I'm relieved to learn milk is what it drinks."

It was now blue dusk outside. I turned on the light and saw that the mouse was all primed and ready for a night of revelry. It didn't seem to miss the tinkling bells, and ran swiftly, purposefully on its wheel. "As if to 'put a girdle round about the earth in forty minutes,'" I said, quoting Puck. Then I prepared my supper of tea and toast, and as I ate, I read.

At my nine-o'clock bedtime, I decided against the previous night's procedure of putting the cage in the bathtub. "I will *not* share it with a mouse," I said with distaste. But since the weather had turned wintry, I could not leave the creature on the sill and open the casements. I could, and most certainly would, turn it over to that gaunt cat soon, for that was its natural fate, but I couldn't let it slowly freeze to death.

I removed the cage to my coffee table, out of any possible icy draft. Before opening the windows, I stood looking at the snow frills on the black iron casement frames. Pretty. What had begun as a dull, dreary, gray day had become the white Christmas that Mr. Gardiner had said his Trudy's intuition had predicted.

Then an odd thought struck me. Animals had become strangely involved with my Christmas: a bird, a dog, a cat, a mouse. Unexpectedly in my imagination rose an image of the stable scene in Bethlehem, with animals bowing before the Christ Child in the manger. But nary a dog, a cat, a bird, or a mouse, I reminded myself, so I, too, can do without them— especially that revolting little rodent.

But, on the whole, Christmas had not been unendurable, though the mouse had brought its disagreeable moments. And it'll bring more, I brooded, for in accepting the loan of the deodorant sand I had opened up a borrowing acquaintance that could lead to heaven only knew what untimely intrusions into my privacy by that weak character downstairs. Because, I thought, as sure as God made little black rodents, she'll be up here the first thing in the morning to have a look at my cat. Perhaps she would bring her caved-in feline. If so, it would afford an easy solution to my mouse problem, for I would let nature take its course—so help me, I would.

As I have indicated previously, it is my custom upon retiring to read awhile to induce sleep. That night I read in *I and Thou,* Martin Buber's treatise on being and relation. "The person becomes conscious of himself as sharing in being, as co-existing, and thus as being. Individuality becomes conscious of itself as being such-and-such and nothing else. The person says, 'I am,' the individual says, 'I am such-and-such.'"

I laid down the book and watched the small black rodent running senselessly on its wheel. I mused, Does it know itself to have being? Does it think to itself, I am a rodent, I am a black mouse. I am a lonely black mouse on Christmas night?

"Oh, for Pete's sake!" Irritated, I turned off the light only to be jolted by the sudden realization that I had spoken out loud. I felt cold with apprehension. I stared into the dark. Had I indeed acquired the habit of solitary persons, as Father Lane had warned me I might, of talking aloud to myself? I had. And I might as well face up to it. For now I realized that all the livelong day I had been muttering and murmuring to myself about the mouse. A mouse was showing me up to myself, exposing my weaknesses.

After that revelation, sleep took to its heels. I

tossed, I turned, as I had done the night before. I thumped my pillows. I longed to hide in unconsciousness. Finally, I was just drifting off—

Then the cage began to squeak.

Now, I am one who cannot endure the dripping of a leaky faucet. The shrill, metallic squeak-squeak of the wheel at every turn drove me frantic. It was as bad as the bells—worse.

"Damn! Damn! Damn!"

I got up and slammed shut the casements, getting wet snow all over my bare feet. Shivering, I went to the sewing-machine cabinet, yanked open a door, and found a can of oil. It was bone dry. I turned to my dressing alcove, fetched out a jar of wrinkle-removing cream, and angrily applied it to the axle of the wheel. Then, as the unperturbed little beast ran and ran, the squeak wore out. The wheel turned smoothly and noiselessly again.

Thank goodness the wrinkle remover was good for something.

Wearily I reopened the windows, got back into bed, and turned off the light. "I'm dog-tired—no, mouse-tired," I muttered grimly, "and I don't give a hang if I do talk to myself. And if, as Martin Buber says, 'Where there is no sharing there is no reality,' then I've had a very real day, for I've shared Christmas with a mouse."

Worn to a frazzle from the experience of sharing, I fell into a deep sleep.

three

The next morning, to my surprise, the Character with the Cat did not invade my privacy. Perhaps she had more perception than I gave her credit for. At any rate, that day and the next and the next passed, and I had no opportunity to donate my mouse to her cat. So daily I administered to the small rodent's needs with resignation and ill-humor.

Previous to its arrival, I had been accustomed to

linger in bed, as there was nothing special to get up for. But now I would wake up with a sense of urgency. At first, unable to recall what it was I had to do, I would turn over and try to sleep again. Then I'd think, Oh, my stars! I've got to get up and clean that darn cage. For although the sand kept the mouse cage odorless for a reasonable length of time, it had its limits. So I would rise with a groan and go about my distasteful mouse chores with a sour face.

Then, one morning, I was annoyed to note that the mouse did not like my odor, either. After I had taken a hot soak in scented water, to remove all possible taint of mouse from myself, and returned to the living room, the mouse came sniffing to the near side of the cage. At my approach, it turned tail and fled to the far side with its back to me.

"So my odor offends it," I said irascibly. "Well, it just can lump it, because there is nothing it can do about it."

All day long the uncomfortable thought pricked at me: that I, detesting the mouse's odor, could do something about it—and I had—but the mouse, detesting mine, had no self-protection. This seemed unfair, and unfairness always galls me. So I searched out various bottles and boxes of leftovers, and applied talcums, toilet waters, and perfumes in succession to myself, and tested each scent on the mouse. All were offensive. It even fled from the expensive scent Gladys had given me for Christmas.

Finally I put on coat, hat, and galoshes and went shopping. Through dirty melting snow I sloshed, or took crowded buses to department stores and elbowed through more crowds, visiting cosmetic counter after cosmetic counter. Feeling like a fool, I sniffed at bottle stoppers that clerks passed slowly under my nose. At last, I found a scent that, in my estimation, a country mouse might like, and I purchased a bottle of a cheap toilet water called New Mown Hay.

On my way home, I detoured to a Third Avenue supermarket. Emerging with my arms overloaded with groceries, I remembered that the deodorant sand in the jar was getting low, so I stopped at a pet shop and bought a big bag of the stuff. On arriving at our building, I shared the elevator with—wouldn't you know it?—the Character with the Cat. This time, it was I who was laden like a pack donkey and she who pressed my floor button for me.

After I had thanked her coolly, I said, "Now I shall be able to return the deodorant sand you so kindly lent to me Christmas Day." I fully expected her to say that she would go up with me then and there so I could give it to her—but really so she could see my pet. But she didn't.

"Oh, don't bother to return it," she said, smiling. "Consider it a Christmas gift from my cat to yours."

After she got off, I was annoyed because I still had not told her what my pet was, but I could not bring myself to admit that I, a mature woman of sound mind, had kept a mouse for nearly two weeks. "I should have asked her to come up and bring her cat, and then let the slaughter take place," I muttered.

For certainly I was not going to keep that bothersome little rodent much longer.

When I entered the apartment, my eyes went at once to the window sill. The mouse was hidden in sleep. I was tempted to shake it out, so I could try the effect of the scent of New Mown Hay, but since I don't like my own sleep disturbed, I waited until evening, when it emerged. It faced up bravely to my odor of New Mown Hay and I was immensely gratified, until I realized I was pleased because I had pleased a mouse. Horrified, I thought, I'm becoming queer, just as Father Lane warned me I might.

The next day, to my consternation, Jane and Peter arrived at my apartment carrying another large square package, and when they unwrapped it, sure enough, it contained another mouse in a cage. "It's for you to take to Father Lane," Jane explained quickly, and I let out a sigh of relief because it was not for me. However, I was astonished at this largess of mice, and said so tartly.

Peter grinned. "Oh, ours was pregnant when we got her, but Mom didn't know it until too late."

"So your mother is unloading the offspring on anyone she can think of," I said. "Well, I doubt the suitability of such a gift to a priest, especially a Jesuit, but"—with some malice—"I'll deliver it to him promptly, this very afternoon."

And, with equal malice, I did so.

In the rectory's small parlor, after I had removed the two thick bath towels that had shielded the little rodent from the blustery January wind, Father Lane looked down in silence at the cage and its occupant, and finally said, "When I was a boy, I teased and teased my mother to let me have some pet mice. But she said firmly, 'No, son, I'm not going to have my house smelling of animals.' Yet cannily I saved up my allowance and bought a pair of white mice. I took them home, but every time I went near my father, he'd roar, 'Go away, boy, you smell of mice!' He took them back to the pet shop and got my money back." Father Lane shook his head sadly. "I had them just two days."

Then, in triumph, he said, "I wonder what my parents would say now to see me with a mouse of my own."

In astonishment I looked at the Reverend John Lane, S.J. I thought, He's had eighteen years of the severe religious education necessary to turn out a Jesuit; he's had countless more years of dealing with people and their dreary sins, so how is it possible for a small boy to survive in his cassock? Yet now from under his bushy, sandy eyebrows his bright blue eyes gleamed with joy at finally achieving the ownership of a mouse! How do some people, I marvelled, keep this wonderful capacity to take pleasure in the things of life, things which to others might seem trite and even disagreeable.

I said in an acid tone, "I see that you are more pleased with your mouse than I am with mine," and he sent me a sharp glance and said, "Then what you said at Christmas was true—you were spending the day with a mouse?"

"It was true, I'm sorry to say."

"Sorry!" He looked incredulous. "But the companionship of one of God's little creatures can be very wonderful and instructive."

I shrugged. "It can be an awful nuisance," I said. "A mouse has disorganized my whole life. I have to get up mornings no matter how I feel to clean its cage, and it's a nasty job. Its wheel sometimes squeaks in the night and disturbs my sleep. I had to go out in the melting snow to— Well, never mind what for," I interrupted myself. I simply would not reveal that I had gone out to buy toilet water scented to please a mouse. I ended plaintively, "I had arranged my life to suit myself, so I could have comfort and privacy, and now everything has been disrupted, and I don't like it."

Father Lane spoke bluntly. "A gradual yielding to the desire for comfort is characteristic of the aging. And it is a selfish indulgence when one arranges one's life to suit oneself and allows no interference from—"

"A mouse?" I inquired. "Well, Father, I do not intend to allow my convenience to be disturbed by a rodent. I refuse to have my life center around a mouse."

"The center of things could be in the mouse," he commented mildly, "and not necessarily in yourself."

I was silent, feeling reprimanded and misunderstood.

Father Lane looked down at the cage and now spoke with wry appreciation. "It was very considerate and clever of you to tie sachet bags of lavender to it.

My mother never thought of such a solution so I could keep my mice."

"There is an even better solution," I said coldly, for his Irish flattery could not so easily salve my hurt feelings, "but I doubt it was obtainable when you were a boy. It's a product of our age of scientific discovery. I brought a glass jar of it."

For a time, we watched his mouse run upon its wheel. It was a golden tan, very slim, very sleek.

"It has an aristocratic appearance," I observed, then added, "and looks not unworthy to take up residence with the Jesuits on Park Avenue."

Father Lane ignored my unpleasantness. "It's a deer mouse," he commented. For a horrified second, I thought he had used an endearment, as Gladys does so often with her bird, but he continued, "You will note that the mouse has rather long, pointed ears, resembling those of a fawn," and relief flowed over me.

"Its name—so the children told me to tell you—is Michael," I said, in a more agreeable tone. "Its surname is Monk-Mouse—hyphenated to befit its swank address, and Monk to befit a church mouse."

Father Lane glanced at me. "That surname was invented by you. Monk-Mouse, eh?" He chuckled. "Well, Michael, little fellow, I'm delighted to welcome you, and glad you brought along your luggage." He nodded toward the jar of sand, the box of sunflower seeds, the wire box, and the bundle of shredded paper I had provided. "I'm very pleased that you plan a long stay with me."

"Mine had better not plan a long stay with me," I said darkly. Father looked at me quickly.

"Why?" he demanded. And ominously I replied, "You'll find out why after you've had yours for a week."

And after you've scrubbed its cage every morning, I thought as I strode off along Park Avenue. But my conscience bothered me, for Father Lane could not possibly have learned much about mice in the two days he'd had them when he was a boy. Well, I had tried to tell him the facts of life with mice, and in return I'd as much as been told that I was a comfort-loving, self-centered female.

"So now let him find out for himself what 'the companionship of one of God's little creatures' amounts to," I muttered, getting onto my Madison Avenue bus.

As I opened my door, the phone was ringing insistently. Father Lane was calling, and his voice was anxious. "Do you know how a mouse should breathe?"

"Through its nose," I answered. "Why do you ask?"

"Because my mouse is panting," Father Lane replied. "He seems sick. Is it possible that Michael got chilled when you brought him?"

"It is not," I said sharply. "You saw me unwrap two thick bath towels from around the cage. It could not possibly have got chilled. What have *you* been doing to it?"

"Just watching him. But he won't run on his wheel. He refuses to take the sunflower seeds I offer him. He just forlornly crawls under the shredded paper, and when I poke at him, he lies there and pants. Michael is—well—dopey."

"It's sleepy," I said impatiently. "For heaven's sake, Father, don't you know that rodents are nocturnal creatures and sleep all day so they can run all night?"

"Oh," he said meekly. "I'm so sorry I've kept Michael awake when he needs his sleep." And he hung up.

"Sorry he's kept Michael awake, indeed!" I said. "He might better apologize for troubling me." Then it crossed my mind that Father Lane referred to his mouse as "he" or "Michael," while I spoke of the rodent as "it." Well, it was an *it* as far as I was concerned. Then, tired to death of mice, I removed my shoes and lay down for a nap.

When I woke, it was twilight. Vaguely I saw my shadowy mouse running swiftly within the wheel's lower treads. I switched on the light, and the little animal stopped so abruptly that the wheel reversed, whirling the mouse completely around within the wheel, so that for a second it was upside down. I laughed outright.

The mouse repeated its performance. And in amazement I thought, Imagine such a small creature catching on to a new idea, learning to repeat a new action so quickly. Had it also repeated the maneuver in order to hear me laugh? I was about to laugh again, then tightened my mouth. The idea! I must indeed be getting queer. Really, I ought to rid myself of the little beast.

However, the next morning, after I had scrubbed

the cage and brought it back to my table, I was aghast to see that the mouse had apparently got rid of *me*. The wire box was empty, its lid lifted. "Now, where the dickens has that little pest gone to?" I murmured. Then, beneath the newspapers that protected the table, I saw a small bulge moving along, and the mouse emerged. I tiptoed nearer, expecting that at sight of me it would hotfoot it to who knew where. It did nothing of the kind. It came trustfully across the table toward me. When I set down the cage, it hopped in, and, immensely pleased, I exclaimed, "Why, my mouse knows me!"

The following morning, I eliminated the bother of shaking the mouse from cage to wire box, and shook it directly onto the table. "There!" I said. "I'll give it some freedom while I'm cleaning its cage."

On my knees by the bathtub as I scrubbed the cage, I wondered how Father Lane was managing with his mouse chores, especially if he had an early Mass to say. Possibly he had enlisted the aid of his altar boys. I grinned reluctantly at the thought of acolytes tending Father Lane's mouse. Then, annoyed, I muttered, "But *I* have to tend *my* mouse *myself*."

When I returned the cage to the table, the mouse was using its nose to lift the edges of the newspaper and slithering in and out between the pages. How different it was from Father Lane's! His—so slim, golden tan, and sleek—was a rather elegant gentlemanly mouse, while mine—so thickset, black, and stodgy—was a plebeian matronly mouse.

Who would have supposed there could be so much

difference between one mouse and another, I marvelled. Certainly a mismatch if they ever came together. Now, what on earth made me think of that? I wondered as the black mouse hopped into the cage.

On subsequent mornings (I was now habitually an early riser), I left the cleaned cage on the table, went about my housework, and trusted the little animal to choose its own time to hide away and sleep. Then I would close the cage, holding the now invisible mouse, and place it on the window sill.

One morning after this procedure, I removed the newspapers from the table as usual, folded them, and placed them on a low chest for later disposal in the incinerator chute. Then I went into my dressing alcove, and as I was brushing my hair, I felt something slither past my foot. I glanced down—and froze. For I saw a mouse. My first swift thought was, It has come to visit my mouse. Two! A pair! Oh, good grief! That opened up horrendous possibilities. Then I noted that this mouse looked familiar—a certain stodginess, a calmness in my presence.

Not to be outdone in composure by a mouse, I quietly fetched the cage, set it on the floor, and the mouse hopped in as if it were glad to get home. I deduced that it had been hidden in the newspapers when I had put them on the chest, then had hopped to the floor—

"You came trustfully looking for me to help you," I said—then realized I had said "you" to a mouse.

I slammed the cage onto the window sill, wishing

the little beast had remained hidden in the newspapers until I had shoved them into the incinerator.

"*That* would put an end to this affair between a mouse and me," I said.

That evening I sat in my rocker trying to get on with Martin Buber's philosophical dissertation. So far, I had gathered that all human living is governed by the various attitudes of each "*I*" toward the "*Its*" in the world and the one "*Thou*" of eternity. Now I read with interest, "The particular '*It*', by entering into the relational event, may become a '*Thou*.' "

I laid down the paperback, and glanced at the particular *It* in my life, a mouse, and made a wry grimace. Then, as I watched it sitting up and washing its face, music came from my radio, a Strauss waltz. The mouse jumped onto its wheel, and as it ran, surely it kept time to the music. When the music stopped, the mouse stopped. When the music began again, the mouse resumed his rhythmic running. The revolving wheel reminded me of the prayer wheels used in Tibet.

I picked up my prayer beads and began saying the rosary, matching my rocking and my prayers to the rhythm of the wheel and the waltz. I had said ten Hail Marys and was saying, "Glory be to the Father and the Son and the Holy Spirit," when I realized that I had a very pleasant sense of being in tune with the music, the mouse, the world, and the universe, a feeling, too, of companionship. "Oh, my stars! Companionship with a mouse!"

I flung aside my rosary. I stood up abruptly. "I'll

not settle down to coexistence with a mouse," I said loudly. "I'll dispose of it immediately to the cat." But en route to the door, I paused. No, there was a more humane way. Jane and Peter were certain to be back soon to see how the mouse was faring, then I'd insist they take it away with them and turn it loose in the country where it belonged.

"It, *it,*" I repeated in irritation. "I can't keep on calling it *it,* even for the short time it is to remain with me. I'll have to give it a name."

I stood in meditation, tapping my chin. Now, let me see. The black mouse reminded me of a widow, a widow reminded me of the widow Judith in the Old Testament, she who had saved her besieged people when the Assyrian army, with chariots, horsemen and archers, numerous as locusts, were encamped about the Israelite city. The widow Judith alone had gone out and entered the tent of the great enemy commander Holofernes. " 'Her sandals ravished his eyes,' " I quoted. " 'Her beauty made his soul captive; with a sword she cut off his head.' "

In some doubt I eyed my black chubby mouse. "Nevertheless," I said firmly, "I christen you the Widow Judith." Then it crossed my mind that the name might not be applicable as to sex either, for I still hadn't the slightest notion whether the mouse was a he or a she.

But it was soon to be revealed to me, in a not unusual manner and with not unusual consequences.

four

Now, in reflecting back over my mice age, I see that I made my first error that Thanksgiving Day on Long Island, when I pretended to be amused by the antics of the children's mouse. My second mistake was in keeping the gift of rodent until we two got to know each other. My third and gravest error was in giving an "it" a name, for the bestowal of a name confers a personality even on a mouse.

So although I had been quite capable of feeding one "it" to another "it" (a cat), or of drowning an "it," or of sending an "it" to Long Island to be turned loose to fend for itself, I now seemed incapable of doing any of these things to an "it" who had a name and who had become a "you" to me. But I still had no intention of settling down to coexist with a mouse, even though my life had subtly changed for the better. "For one thing," I told myself one evening, "I'm not talking to myself any more. I'm talking to a mouse."

It was on that evening that the small pulpy woman entered my life again. I was returning from the corner newsstand with a paper, and as I entered our building, she came in, too. Smiling rather timidly, as if not certain how I would respond, she asked about my cat. In a dry tone, I told her I was surprised that she had not yet come up to see it, and she said softly, oh, she knew how some women felt about becoming friendly with other women living in the same building. "As I told you," she said, "I'm sensitive and intuitive, and I felt that you are one of those reserved, self-sufficient characters who don't want idle women dropping in on them to talk and talk and talk." Then she smiled, looking at me covertly. "I'm waiting to be invited."

I thought I might as well get it over with, so I asked her to come on up with me. Let her find out how reliable her much-vaunted intuition is when she sees what species of animal was foisted upon me at Christmas against my will, I thought caustically.

When she saw, she exclaimed, "A mouse!" and

burst into unrestrained laughter. "I never said it was a cat—*you* did," I reminded her. "You and your intuition!"

"Yes, me and my intuition," she said, scoffing at herself. "But it certainly was sweet of you not to wound my pride in my sixth sense by telling me it wasn't a cat but a mouse you'd come to borrow the sand for."

"I hadn't come to borrow," I corrected. "I came to offer the mouse as a Christmas dinner for your lean and hungry cat."

"My cat is *not* hungry." She puffed up like an offended Bantam hen. "He eats voraciously and stays thin as a rail, while I eat very sparingly and grow fat as a partridge." What clichés she uses, I thought. "Plump," I said courteously.

"Fat," she contradicted calmly. "Oh, I'm not afraid of a true word." Then an acquisitive glint came into her green eyes. "Does the offer of a free meal for my cat still stand?" She watched the rotund mouse taking its evening constitutional on the wheel, and I felt unexpected trepidation. Then she turned back to me. "Have you given the mouse a name yet?"

"Yes. The Widow Judith."

"Because it's a lone black mouse. How sweet." She sighed. "I think it must be just lovely to be a widow." She paused. "Well, now that it has a name, we can't condemn the Widow Judith to being only meat, can we?" Then, to my surprise, she winked at me—a gay, roguish wink. "Not until she has had her fling—for, of course, you'll get a mate for her in the spring."

"I shall not!" I cried, horrified.

"You ought to," she urged. "Especially in the spring. And mice propagate fabulously. In no time, you would have myriads of sweet, tiny baby mice."

I shivered involuntarily. "I cannot imagine any possible circumstances that would induce me to admit into my home another mouse—especially one of the male sex."

She looked at me, her green eyes thoughtful, and then asked, "Mind if I look about your orderly apartment? Mine is always such a mess."

As she walked delicately about, I thought, She is as curious as a cat, and she certainly does move like one. She was not at all on a par with the cultured, intelligent women who had been my friends in the past. On the contrary, I reflected, she is ordinary in mentality, personality, and character. And I ought to know, for I am an excellent judge of character.

Or I was once, I thought dubiously, for I remembered that at Christmas I had taken this woman to be a person of no family or cultural background, and then had walked into her living room to find it crammed with heirlooms. Have I become so out of touch with humanity, I asked myself, that I can no longer estimate people correctly? The possibility disquieted me. But, at any rate, her appearance alone was enough to discourage any likelihood of our friendship. That dreadful cropped orange hair—

"I dyed my hair to match my cat—remember?" she said over her shoulder, surprising me. "Why don't you dye yours to match your mouse? You'd look sweet with black hair, especially if you left one white streak. It would add distinction to your appearance."

She doesn't like my looks either, I thought resentfully. She thinks *me* commonplace-looking.

Then, catching sight of the paperback book on my table, she let out a squeal of astonishment. "Don't tell me *you* are reading Martin Buber!"

"I'm trying to," I said coldly. "But his philosophy is too involved for my limited intelligence."

"Involved? Oh, my dear! Understanding it is as easy as falling off the water wagon. Listen and I'll explain it to you. It is merely that everybody ought to become chummy with everybody else—and with all things and animals—and that we ought to see right through people—things—and animals—straight into God and all His creation." She smiled encouragingly at me. "What's involved about that?" She picked up the book. "Have you come to the place where he tells about looking into his cat's eyes? Well, his cat's eyes seemed to ask him, 'Is it possible that you think of me? Do you really not just want me to have fun? Do I concern you? Do I exist in your sight?' " She looked shyly at me. "I look into my cat's eyes and my cat looks into mine, we exchange very meaningful glances, my cat and I. In fact, we have established relation."

I was as surprised now to hear her quote Martin Buber as I had been at Christmastime when she quoted Shakespeare. She is full of surprises, I thought —but perhaps many humans are, and I have forgotten it since I broke off communication with the world.

Then her eyes flicked to the window sill and she inquired slyly in her purring voice, "Do *you* exchange glances with your mouse? Do *you* ever look into your mouse's eyes, and your mouse into yours?"

My ire rose. She knows quite well it can't be done, I thought. She walks like a cat, she has a feline's softness, and she can use her claws, too. Now I felt an intense dislike for her and hoped her intuition would tell her so.

"Well, never mind, dear," she said consolingly. "Just having something to do for—even if it's only a mouse—will keep a woman calm and contented. I know. And I'm a very feminine woman."

Feminine, my eye! I thought bitterly. You're female—more female than most women.

Then she pussyfooted to the shelves of books that cover one end of my living room. Running her pudgy white hand along them, she said, "What a lot of nice, falling-apart, shabby old books. They look *used*. And if there's one thing I can't stand, it's unused things. Maybe because I'm an old maid. Anyway, when I see books in new-looking, shiny bindings, I know that the pages inside are probably uncut. Oh-oh! Here's a set of 'The Arabian Nights'—unexpurgated! Hurrah!"

She took out a volume, riffled its pages avidly, and said, "I'm looking for the unexpurgated parts."

I did not suggest that she sit down to find them, and finally she asked diffidently, "May I borrow this Book Three?"

"Take it and welcome," I said aloud, and inwardly, but go—for heaven's sake, go!

Book in hand, she drifted toward the door, which I willingly held open for her. As she left, she turned and said warmly, "It's so nice we've become friends after all these years of living in the same building and barely speaking, isn't it, Mrs. Wood? I know your name because I looked for it on your mailbox, but I imagine you didn't look for mine—it's Julia Tate. Grandmother always called me Gentle Julia. I'm still Miss, but you're a widow, aren't you—like your mouse? So maybe you *can* establish relation with her, even though you and the mouse can't look into each other's eyes."

Just as I was thinking wearily, She's one of those doorway loiterers, she went briskly off, calling over her shoulder, "Thanks for inviting me up and lending me this book. Have a pleasant evening with the Widow Judith."

I watched her to the elevator. There she joined another of my bowing acquaintances, an over-tall young wife who lives in a large apartment at the end of the corridor on my floor. We bowed now. Her two children were with her—a lanky dark-haired lad of about ten and a quick-eyed little blond girl, possibly six, whose names I had never troubled to learn. Chattering and laughing, they all entered the elevator together, and I closed my door relieved that now, at last, I could read my evening paper in peace.

But before I settled down to it, I went to the window sill to stare pensively at my mouse. What that character Gentle Julia had brought to my attention was true: I had never looked into the eyes of my mouse, and it had never looked into mine. There had never been that startled recognition in glance on glance to establish relation between us.

I felt a sudden isolation, an aching loneliness. This mouse, I mused, can see only an infinitesimal part of me—a bit. To the mouse, I must seem a prodigious being, a giantess. "How is it possible," I murmured in wonder, "for such a small creature not to be in mortal terror of my enormous self? How is it possible to recognize me—to trust me—to rely on me for food, for its very life?" Did I exude, along with the scent of new-mown hay, an odor of friendliness?

I doubted it.

Certainly I had not exuded even a decent hospitality toward my recently departed caller—a being of my own size and kind. I had not asked her to sit down or offered her a drink—even of water, though when I had called upon her, uninvited, she had offered me a glass of sherry—and gulped down two herself, I remembered. This evening, I had smelled liquor on her breath, too. It was the soft, pliable, sensitive women who became solitary drinkers when lonely.

"When lonely"—the words echoed in my mind. Neither today nor at Christmastime had I put myself out one iota to relieve her loneliness or that of Gladys. But I pushed this fact aside. "It's their problem, not mine," I muttered.

Hadn't I, out of consideration, arranged my own life so I would never become a problem to others? Surely I had the right to protect myself from the problems of other people, I argued. Anyway, I had not been completely discourteous to Miss Tate. I had lent her a book.

And that gives her a good excuse to come again to return it, I thought gloomily. Well, when I had accepted the loan of the Kleen-Cat sand, I had known that it would open up the way to a borrowing acquaintance; now it had begun. I could expect all sorts of untimely interruptions to the writing of my memoirs.

The next day, at noon, an imperative knock sounded at my door. "Just as I expected," I grumbled, but when I opened the inner door, I was confronted from beyond the screen door by the two children who live down the hall. I should have known that Gentle Julia was a newsmonger.

"We wanna come in to see your mouse," shouted the lanky lad, and his loud voice hurt my ears, for I am sensitive to noise.

I said discouragingly, "A mouse is a nocturnal creature. It hides away all day to sleep."

"Then we'll come in and see where the mouse hides to sleep," said the little girl just as loudly. "O.K?"

There seemed to be nothing to do but to admit them. I unhooked the screen door. They ran in and crossed to the window to stare at the nest of shredded paper where the mouse slept. Since I had remained standing at the door, they got the idea and soon went out docilely enough. But in the hall the boy turned back to shout, "We'll have to keep coming in until we catch your mouse awake and running on its wheel!"

"O.K.?" yelled the little girl.

"It is *not* O.K.," I said harshly. "And stop shouting at me. I'm not deaf, as you seem to think." Then I explained, in a kindlier tone, "It is not O.K., because the mouse runs on its wheel only at night, after all children are in bed asleep."

Gravely they thought this over; the small blond girl studied me with eyes the color of violets and the dark boy with eyes like black olives. How different the two were in appearance, I thought. They departed and I closed the doors, relieved because the children had so readily accepted the impossibility of seeing the rodent.

Late that evening, I prepared to retire. I had cold-creamed my face, put up my front hair on curlers, and was applying a frown-removing plaster when a discreet knock on the screen door made me pause. Now, I wondered, who on earth could that be? No one had knocked on my door at night since Christmas Eve.

I tiptoed out into the living room. The cover had been removed from my studio couch, the bedclothes turned back, and the pillows heaped up preparatory to my reading myself to sleep. The knock was repeated more urgently.

I won't answer, I thought; I'll pretend I'm not home. But possibly a line of light showed underneath my doors. I opened the inner one a crack, then wished to heaven I hadn't.

For, with acute dismay, I saw outside a small crowd waiting to be admitted.

five

Through my screen door I saw standing in the hall, the two children, their over-tall mother, and their even taller father. There they were—the whole family who lived at the end of the hall, whose names I had never bothered to learn.

"Mom let us stay up late so we could come over to see your mouse running on its wheel," announced the boy at the top of his voice.

"Mom and Dad wanna see it, too," the little girl cried.

The mother, who had dark curly hair, smiled down from her lofty height. "We're the Blackburns," she said. "If our call is inconvenient for you, Mrs. Wood—?"

"Not at all," I replied with the scant courtesy of a woman caught in a frayed bathrobe, hair rollers, and cold-creamed face. Surreptitiously I removed the wrinkle plaster from my brow, thinking resentfully, She might at least have had the decency to phone— and grudgingly opened my two doors to admit them.

As they trooped in, last of all the towering father, I wondered, How did she ever find a man taller than she to marry? I spoke in a parched tone. "Pardon my unconventional appearance and the disarray of this room, but I was about to retire," adding hastily, "early, because I felt a head cold coming on."

"I always go to bed early, too, when I'm all alone and don't know what to do with myself." A slow smile accompanied the mother's drawl. She seemed unaware of my chilly reception. "D'ya know what? When that nice old maid Miss Tate told the children you had a mouse, I could hardly believe my ears. It's usually children who have mice for pets."

Undoubtedly she thought I was in my second childhood. I spoke stiffly. "Some people have greatness— some have mice—thrust upon them," I said, and thanked heaven that the plural was used only figuratively.

She folded her slender height into my armchair as

if preparing to stay awhile; in leisurely fashion, she brought out a pack of cigarettes and offered me one, which I declined. As she lit hers, I noticed that her face was as unlined as a china egg. Had mine ever been that smooth? She glanced toward the window sill where the Widow Judith was running contentedly on her wheel and the children were laughing and shouting as if their vocal cords were made of steel.

"Sandy, stop your yellin'," she said lazily, as if she didn't much care whether he obeyed or not. "Peggy, stop your jumpin' up and down, or that grouchy woman downstairs will complain to the landlord again." She smiled her slow smile at me. "Some folks just can't understand that children have to behave like children. But I thank God they do."

"But, Sis, honey, some folks aren't used to such an unholy racket," her husband reminded her. Standing next to me, he was so tall that he brought to mind the cedars of Lebanon, whose tops touched the clouds. He had deep-set, thoughtful eyes, and his hair was crew-cut. Thrusting his big bony hands deep into his coat pockets, he said, "Why don't we turn this place over to the kids and the mouse, and take Mrs. Wood over to our place for a drink?" He grinned down at me. "It'll be good for your head cold."

I could have done with a drink—head cold or not, but I declined in economical syllables, "No, thank you."

He didn't press the invitation but said pleasantly, "Well, another time, and soon. We'll be counting on it."

Then I realized that he had remained standing because I had, and I sat down abruptly on the edge of a straight chair. He made himself comfortable on my couch, stretched out his long legs before him, and eyed his big feet. "When I was a lad in Kentucky," he said, "I kept a pair of pet mice in our tobacco shed. But I wasn't allowed to bring them anywhere near our house because of the smell, as y'all can surmise."

"There's no smell of mouse in here," his wife observed, "because Miss Tate introduced Mrs. Wood to Kleen-Cat, and lent her some."

My private affairs are fast becoming public, I thought in resentment, thanks to Gentle Julia's wagging tongue.

The father spoke over the children's screams of laughter. "Your mouse looks lonely," he said. "You ought to have a pair. Would you like me to get you another?"

"Certainly not," I said shortly. "One is more than sufficient."

"What did you say?" he asked loudly, then, turning to his wife, "To carry on a conversation in the same room with those kids is impossible." He rose to his great height. "I'll take them home and put them to bed so you and Mrs. Wood can yakkatayak in peace and quiet and get really acquainted."

As he went out, dragging the protesting girl and boy each by a hand, their mother said fondly, "Aren't they little monsters? They're adopted, you know."

I had not known, but it seemed immaterial then.

She lit another cigarette from the butt she was about to discard. "We adopted them when they were only tiny, red-wrinkled, adorable infants. Now we're in the process of adopting another—a baby boy we intend to name Robert, after my husband. And I hope to goodness he'll grow up to be as tall—so some big, ungainly gal like me can nab him for a husband, and won't be miserable because of her outsize."

"I suppose being so tall is—was a problem," I replied, feeling a faint sympathy rising in me.

Then she wrinkled her nose in my direction and sniffed. "I keep thinking I smell the odor of fresh hay."

With dismay and feeling impelled to explain, I said stiffly, "When I perceived that the rodent disliked my—er—usual odor as much as I disliked that of a mouse, it struck me as unfair that I could take adequate means to protect myself but the mouse could not. So I experimented with various scents until I found one that the mouse could endure."

Amused, she glanced at me with her warm brown eyes. "Now, that was mighty nice of you. Most folks wouldn't have bothered to please a mouse."

She thinks I'm in my dotage—a character, I thought. It would have been better to let her believe I was the sort of person who used strong scent to please myself, rather than to tell her I used it to please a mouse. Why had I explained? The latent resentment I felt at the evening's interruption, which had been smoldering like a wet fire, now flared up. I rose abruptly. "If you'll excuse me—"

She took her departure at once.

As I wearily emptied her ashtray, I muttered, "It's evident she's a chain smoker, and lazy to boot. Southern women usually are." Henceforth I'd probably have to put up with ill-timed visits from her and her noisy, undisciplined children. Because, I reflected despairingly, it was going to be difficult to return to a coolly bowing acquaintance with people who, nameless, had meant nothing to me, but whose family name I now knew to be Blackburn, and whose children Sandy and Peggy, adopted, were now known personalities. Against the usual run-of-the-mill children I might have kept my doors closed, but I doubted that I could shut out adopted ones.

"And it's your fault," I accused the Widow Judith as I placed her cage on the coffee table for the night. I scowled down at the mouse running fruitlessly on her wheel, then sighed and said, "So do we all run much of our lives."

But I had reached a pause in my life; I had withdrawn into a place of privacy and quiet, which now seemed in danger of being nibbled away. "Still I shall maintain my barriers and keep my reserves inviolable," I said decisively. "I have no intention of rejoining the mouse race or permitting it to rejoin me."

In my dressing alcove, I applied a fresh frown-removing plaster to my scowl, then returned to the living room to open the casement windows. It was sleeting outside. Feeling low in my mind and insecure in my privacy, I went to bed.

The next day, in the late afternoon, a pale descending sun came out while I was returning from the supermarket. As I picked my way carefully along the icy sidewalk in front of the Catholic Charities Building, Father Lane emerged from the entrance, took off his hat, and looked pleased at our chance encounter. "And how are you and your mouse getting along together?" he inquired cheerily.

"We're enduring each other," I replied. "Put your hat back on, Father, or you'll catch your death." As he did so, I added, "I admit I'm surprised at the ingenuity of such a small creature. Why, this morning the mouse used its tiny nose to lift the gate of the cage, and escaped to run about on the window sill among the plants. And then—"

"I'm due on a sick call." Father Lane glanced at his wristwatch, but nonetheless he lingered to talk of *his* mouse. "Michael shows intelligence, too—and an urge for liberty. One evening, I felt compassion for the caged little creature, so I took a deep drawer out of my bureau, dumped out its contents and put the cage inside, and let Michael out to scamper in this spacious yard. I thought it was quite safe, but next morning when I got up and looked into the drawer—no mouse!"

"Didn't you know a mouse can climb a wall?" I demanded, and, chuckling, he replied, "I do now." He went on, "Well, I was scheduled to say an early Mass, but first I had to locate the errant Michael. I looked high and low—under the bureau—behind it— behind my chair cushions—under the radiator. Imagine my predicament!"

I imagined it—the sleep-rumpled priest in his pajamas, frantically hunting for his mouse. He was now saying, "It was imperative that I find Michael, for another mouse has occasionally been seen in the rectory and in the church, and with Michael at liberty—" He rubbed his cold red nose. "Well, there was no telling what that mouse might start."

"What!" I exclaimed. "A church mouse—with his vow of chastity?"

Father Lane got his religious dander up. He sent me a severe glance. "You must not joke about Holy Orders," he said sternly. Then he became human again. "Well, as I was searching everywhere, I heard papers rattle on my desk, and when I looked, there was that little imp sampling my next sermon." Father Lane chuckled again. And if I were to describe Father Lane in one sentence, I'd say he is a chuckling priest. "Michael liked it, too," he added. "He had nibbled it to bits."

I remarked dryly, "When Gladys Hall, an Episcopalian acquaintance of mine, dines with me tonight, I'll tell her that she must attend your church next Sunday to hear a certain Jesuit's sermon, as it has the approval of his mouse."

"No!" Father Lane said sharply. "I prefer that you do not mention that I have a pet mouse." Then, loftily, "An Episcopalian might not understand it."

As I left Father Lane, I reflected that he, too, was probably being taunted for having a pet usually associated with children. Then I thought sulkily, He showed only a tepid interest in the mouse in *my* possession, but he was ready enough to talk about *his*. All that recounting of the search for his mouse. And how naïve was Father's relief that he had recovered Michael in ample time to prevent something plural starting in the rectory.

When I entered our building, I met Mr. Gardiner, thin and stooped, returning from walking his prescient mongrel. I hadn't encountered them since Christmas Eve.

He greeted me with mild jocosity. "*You* don't have to walk *your* pet on a leash," he said, and I knew that the news was spreading. As we went up in the elevator, he picked his teeth with the ever-present toothpick, then said, "Hanged if I can understand what satisfaction you get from a mouse. It can't bark and it can't wag its tail when you arrive home."

I held stonily silent. Then he confided, "When I was a little shaver, I wanted a pair of mice, the way all kids do." He glanced in commiseration at me, as if I were a case of retarded mentality. Then he lifted his dog in his arms and scratched her ears. "I doubt Trudy has ever seen a mouse. Mind if we go up with you now to see yours?"

"It isn't convenient," I said shortly. "I'm expecting a guest for dinner."

"Oh, we'll only stay a moment," he persisted, putting the dog down. "Here, let me carry those groceries for you." But I was adamant. "No, thank you," I said, and he got off the elevator, looking rebuffed.

As I went on up, I thought, Maybe a wag and a bark are not enough for him, maybe he needs conversation. But what could we possibly converse about —I and that nondescript, aging bachelor, with his faded thin hair and washed-out eyes? He had the protective coloring of a man whose need was to blend in with his background. Yet he would not blend into the background of my mind; he stood out annoyingly, with a hurt, baffled look on his face.

So I was in a bad mood when I prepared dinner for Gladys—and unwillingly, for she had invited herself. Only that morning she had called, her strident voice reverberating in the phone receiver. "I say! I haven't seen you since the day before Christmas, which, by the way, was not a merry one. I'm coming to dinner tonight, yes, I am, and don't say no. If you're afraid I'll keep you up past your usual bedtime, make the dinner an early one, but I'm coming. And, don't worry, I shan't bring Armstrong-Jones. I'll leave the darling bird at home. I'm invading your privacy, love, but I'll not make it unhygienic. Don't go to any bother, meat and potatoes with a spot of tea will do. I'll bring some of the fruitcake you gave me for Christmas as dessert. Ta-ta."

I hung up, feeling drenched with words. Why did women like Gladys, who lived alone, develop the atrocious habit of talking incessantly without listening to others? And need she twit me about my preference for cleanliness, privacy, and keeping early hours?

Now as I went about setting my table for two, I dreaded her arrival. And what will she say when she sees my mouse, I wondered. Then I stood stock-still.

I had said, "*my* mouse," and was reminded of what I'd read that afternoon in the Buber paperback. It was something disparaging about a Self who over-emphasized its *my*—"my kind—my race—my creation." Now I realized how I overemphasized the *my:* my independence—my privacy—my home—my books—my plants.

I had just said, *my* mouse.

Biting my lips, I continued setting the table in preparation for Gladys's arrival.

six

With the dinner table in readiness, I braced myself for my guest's arrival and avalanche of words. She came in, dramatically threw off her thrift-shop mink coat and revealed her too tight, too short gold lamé sheath. I knew what her first outburst would be and it was.

"A mouse! Oh, I say! I never thought to see *you* with any pet! But a mouse! My word!"

The rodent had again escaped from the cage to run about on the window sill, in and out among the plants.

"I say!" Gladys cried in her stagey voice. "You wouldn't come to Christmas dinner with me and Sweety-Tweety because you were too fastidious. 'Unhygienic' you pronounced, looking down your nose at my bird. Now see who's sharing her sanitary privacy with a mouse and is content to do so," she jeered.

"The mouse is not on my dinner table nor will it ever be," I replied dispassionately. "And that I'm content is your own surmise."

After dinner, as we had tea, I informed her of how the mouse had entered my life. When I finished, she said, "I'm astonished you didn't extirpate it on the spot—that you kept it even for a day. Well, I hope you keep it indefinitely. Perhaps it will make you more human, because if you ask me, you're becoming too much of a recluse."

"I didn't ask you," I replied.

Unperturbed, she poured herself a second cup of strong tea. "Of course, all pets are pests," she conceded. "Goodness knows, owning them has disadvantages we have to put up with in exchange for their company. Yet I must say I don't see what company a mouse can be. It's much smaller than a bird—it can't fly about—it can't sing and make a joyful noise. Come to think of it, have you ever even heard it squeak?"

Come to think of it, I hadn't. But I replied knowingly, "A mouse squeaks upon occasion." What the occasions were, I didn't know then, but I was soon to learn one of them. Now I was annoyed with Gladys, for she was another who felt impelled to tell me what my mouse could *not* do. Gentle Julia had told me the mouse could not look into my eyes. Mr. Gardiner had told me the mouse could not bark or wag its tail. And now Gladys told me the mouse could not make a joyful noise. I wished peevishly she would go home.

She intercepted my glance at the clock. "Your bedtime, eh? Oh, I say, it's only curtain time in the theatres. My many years on the stage accustomed me to late hours."

"I was never on the stage," I said.

Calmly she poured another cup of tea, this time for me. "It'll keep you awake, and staying up late one night won't kill you. I feel like talking."

When *didn't* she? I asked myself. She had not my capacity for solitude; she needed an audience and a large stage, for her gestures were wide and dramatic, her voice self-amplified. In my small apartment, she seemed to take up more than her fair share of space and oxygen. Her appearance demanded too much attention as well—that dyed red hair, those gray eyes heavy with black makeup. Then, as she talked and talked and talked, I wandered off into my own thoughts.

Tomorrow I'd get down to my memoirs again. I'd write an account of the time in Paris, after the First World War, when I was a guest of White Russian émigrés at an Eastern-rite Easter breakfast. I had sat next to Prince Y——, who, it was said, had been in the plot that resulted in the stabbing of Rasputin—

"I say! You're not listening to a word I say," Gladys cried. "You're like all women who live alone. You've lost the art of listening. You sneak off into your cozy mental boudoir filled with memories and let real life pass you by."

She rose irately, "I'll leave you with your silent spooks, I'm going home to my singing bird." Putting on her coat, she went on unpleasantly, "No doubt you feel very superior behind your iron curtain of two doors, in your closed society of '*my* privacy, *my* independence, *my* pride, *my* home, *my* books, *my* plants and *my* memories.' And now 'my mouse.'"

She made a dramatic exit but turned to say, "The vanishing years have filched your sociability. If you ask me, you're now only fit company for a mute mouse. Good night."

Later, preparing for bed, I felt bone-tired, sick at heart, and generally wretched. Everybody seemed bent upon pointing out to me not only the deficiencies in my mouse but in myself. Yet, I thought, if it is true that it was only without grace that I admitted people into my home and my life, still it was my life, and surely I had a right to live it as I chose.

In my bed, I turned over and over for what seemed endless time, and finally I knew that there was imperative need for me to see my spiritual director. I resolved that on the next day, the very first thing, I would go and have a talk with him.

Then I went to sleep.

But it was late afternoon before I entered the rectory. The elderly woman at the reception desk announced me, then turned from the house phone to say, "Father wishes you to go up to the second floor to the school assembly hall." As I climbed the broad creaking stairs, I wondered why Father Lane did not receive me, as usual, in one of the small parlors downstairs. When I entered the assembly hall, it was vacant, except for row after row of maple desk-arm chairs.

I was laying aside my coat when I heard cautious footsteps and Father Lane entered, his black cassock flapping about his legs. Holding something concealed behind his back, he looked about to make sure he was unobserved, then spoke guardedly. "I thought you might like to see Michael Monk-Mouse," he said, and brought the cage into view.

With difficulty I refrained from saying snappishly that I had enough mouse at home. He placed the cage on the broad arm of my chair, sat himself down in the adjoining one, and said in a pleased voice, "Michael knows me now. He takes sunflower seeds right out of my hand." He offered the slim tan mouse a seed, then glanced briefly at me.

"Well?" he said, and waited for me to tell him what was troubling me.

I said plaintively, "I thought I had my life well-organized. I had accepted the limitations of late-middle age—the demise of lifelong friends—the inadvisability of cultivating new ones. I had—"

"Look!" Father Lane cried excitedly, then added in disappointment, "Oh, you were too late. You missed seeing Michael take a seed from my fingers." Then he glanced at me apologetically. "I interrupted you. I'm sorry."

I bit my lip in vexation and began again, with an

edge to my voice. "I had resigned myself to a quiet, solitary life. Indeed, I've grown to prefer it. I've lived as I think a sensible older woman should."

"The world is not a sensible place," Father commented dryly, "and if you act sensibly, you get out of step. I've tried before to make you see that you have dissociated yourself from life and people to your own detriment."

"You have scolded me often enough for living to myself, yes," I grumbled, and he replied, "So I should, for the ingrown person becomes cut off from human relationships, and that is unhealthy—and unchristian."

"But surely I've the right to pick and choose the people with whom to establish relation," I insisted. "I don't have to permit my privacy to be invaded by a lot of common people who grate on my nerves."

Father Lane offered his mouse another seed before he asked, "What common people?"

"Oh, there's a pristine maiden lady living on the floor below me who searches out the unexpurgated parts in *The Arabian Nights*. Of course, she also reads Martin Buber. I want to be fair. But she tries to bleach out her loneliness in a wash of wine. She hangs her feelings out on a line to be tattered by every ill wind that blows. She coddles what she calls her 'hypersensitivity.' She's a clinging vine if ever I saw one, and her tendrils are reaching out toward me. But so far I've managed to evade them. She lives with a cat she treats as an equal."

"Ah, so she understands that one has a responsibility to God even for an attitude toward a cat." Father

Lane nodded approvingly. "She sounds to me like a very appealing, feminine woman. Possibly you have grown out of touch and sympathy with human frail— Oh, oh, look!" Father Lane's grave, sacerdotal tone rose into one of boyish excitement. Then he said, in a letdown voice, "You missed seeing Michael whirl clear around inside his wheel. For a second, he was upside down and he looked so comical." He chuckled, then demanded, "Well, who else has disrupted your carefully tidy life?"

His description of my sane life further annoyed me, but I concealed it and said, "A set of ungainly parents —Southerners. They're easygoing and inconsiderate of others. They bring in their noisy, undisciplined children when I am ready to retire. Then, there's a vulgar bachelor who picks his teeth in the elevator on the way out to walk his mongrel dog. There's a pseudo-British ex-actress who spouts trite English expressions and invites herself to dinner and keeps me up late."

"Umm. It takes humor and courage to accept people as they are," Father Lane commented. Now he looked directly at me with a sharp, clinical glance. "You have the look of a woman who fears that her money is all gone. Was privacy such a treasure?"

Not waiting for my reply, he asked another question. "Why have all these people invaded your seclusion?"

"They come in to see the mouse," I replied angrily. "That mouse brings them in."

"So a mouse has cracked your reinforced concrete world, eh?" Father Lane chuckled deeply.

Nettled, I replied, "Yes, my life is being disrupted by a mouse, and it's absurd that anything so small—"

"A mouse is not so small as the Host in which our Lord dwells," Father Lane said matter-of-factly.

I thought that irrelevant and irreverent and ignored it. I said, "I'd hoped that I was done with the world and its troublesome inhabitants."

He nodded. "I know, but you've been missing the experience of life itself, though you are still on the hither side of eternity and still a vital woman—and a very handsome one, too."

"And one not susceptible to the flattery of an Irish Jesuit," I said disagreeably. "A woman who cannot be soft-soaped into relinquishing her secluded life."

Father Lane looked meditative and murmured, "Where there is danger, the rescuing force appears," Then he lifted the cage up to the level of his eyes and said to his mouse, "You are not so foolish, are you, Michael? You know that life must be lived, worked and suffered up to its very end, even if there's nothing to do but run upon a wheel."

I gave up. I rose in a fume and put on my coat. "With that mouse between us, Father, it is impossible for me to discuss my problem with you to any advantage."

As I walked off along Park Avenue, I thought aggrievedly, Father Lane is no help at all in restoring peace to my life and soul. And I returned home with a baffled feeling that my destiny was unaccountably and inextricably entangled with mice.

seven

As winter passed, my life became more and more disorganized. As I had feared, it was difficult to keep my doors shut against the adopted children. Sandy and Peggy knocked at all sorts of hours, inopportune for me but opportune for them—mornings as they went off to school, noontimes when they came home for lunch, afternoons after school—on the off chance that they might catch the mouse awake and running on its wheel.

Once, I said in exasperation, "I've told you again and again that the mouse hides away to sleep all day." Peggy popped her gum and answered, "But, just like us kids wake up thirsty for a drink of water, a mouse might," and Sandy added, "And come out to get it." Sometimes this had happened, but I wouldn't tell the children so. I shut the door emphatically and returned to my interrupted memoirs.

One Saturday, as I was writing, I ignored the pounding on my screen door as long as I could, but finally I jerked open the inner door. The two children grinned at me through the screen door. But I said irritably, "There's no earthly use for you to come in. The Widow Judith is awake only very early in the morning, before you children get up. She runs about on my table while I scrub her cage."

This last bit of information was a slip of the tongue.

Peggy eyed me from beneath her thick bangs. "Mom let us stay up late one night to see your mouse, and so—"

"So she'll let us get up early to see your mouse run around on the table," Sandy said, bouncing a ball. Then Peggy advised, "But you better phone and ask Mom to let us, or she'll say"—she mimicked her mother's drawl—" 'Now, y'all mustn't be a pest to Mrs. Wood.' "

With the desperate hope of ending these intrusions, I phoned their mother. She protested, "But tomorrow's Sunday, and Robert and I like to sleep late."

"So sleep late," I replied tartly. "I was not suggesting that you and your husband come over. Let the children run down the corridor in their pajamas and bedroom slippers."

As I hung up, Peggy shrieked, "Yippee! A pajama party!" Sandy yelled, "Whoopee! A surprise breakfast party for the mouse!"

"That it's to include breakfast is a surprise to me," I said dryly. "Now, for heaven's sake go away, and don't knock again today."

They complied. So I finished writing an account of the time I was kissed, when I was a young girl, by a Nobel Prize winner at a literary cocktail party. But it was not until I had wrestled with my conscience that I added the truth—that he was intoxicated at the time and did not know whom he was kissing.

The next morning (although I, too, like to sleep late on Sunday), I got up groggily while it was still pitch dark so I could make preparations in peace before the children arrived. After the cage had been scrubbed, I varied my usual routine by trying to shoo the Widow Judith into it immediately. But she was accustomed to a morning gambol and refused to be deprived of it. After pursuing the fleet, stubborn little rodent around the table several times, I finally lunged, grabbed her tail, and swung the black mouse unceremoniously into the cage.

I had removed the soiled newspapers and was laying a plastic breakfast cover before I realized that I had touched a mouse. I had grabbed the prehensile tail. And a long, slow, cold shiver passed through me. All in a tremor, I hurried to wash my hands. "I picked up a mouse," I murmured incredulously, and felt as if another side of me were coming up for air—a side of me I had not known.

As I resumed setting the table, the outraged mouse rattled the cage gate, demanding to be let out again. "Hold your horses," I said crossly, laying four places. At each child's place I set a glass of milk and an empty cereal bowl. Nearby I placed several small boxes of cereal, hoping that the children would each find one they liked. Then, feeling like a nincompoop, I set a place for the mouse—a tin bottle cap full of milk, and for a cereal bowl I filled my silver thimble with raw oatmeal.

Morning's cold gray light was awash over the casement windows before I sat down wearily to fortify myself for the coming ordeal with a cup of strong coffee. I was only half fortified when I heard the children tugging at the screen door and their excited yells, "It's us! It's us!"

Quickly I opened the cage and went to open the inner door. "Shh!" I warned. "Do you want to wake up the whole building? Calm down."

Sandy and Peggy, dressed in rumpled pajamas, burst in carrying their slippers. They squirmed onto their chairs, laughing hilariously to see the Widow Judith trotting about on the table, unafraid. She ambled up onto the saucers to peer curiously into the cereal bowls. After some inspection, she decided, to each his own, and trotted to the silver thimble, selected a flake of oatmeal, and sat up, munching it contentedly.

Peggy shook her finger at the mouse. "Now, you mustn't eat till we say thanks to Him," she said, pointing skyward. I said to Sandy "You say grace," and after he had, I thanked God silently and fervently that Gladys was not there to witness what was on my breakfast table.

After a time, during which the children and the mouse ate their cereal and became acquainted, Peggy leaned back, let out an ecstatic breath, and said, "This is the very, *very* first time we've ever, *ever* had breakfast with a mouse."

"It's a first time for me, too," I said crustily, "and now it's over." I rose. "And if the mouse knows it's time to go into her cage and hide away to sleep, you Protestant children ought to know it's time to go home and get ready to go to your Sunday school, so scoot! I must dress and hurry to Mass."

The next day, it happened that I went down in the elevator with their towering mother. She spoke down to me in her lazy way. "That was a mighty wonderful thing you did for my young ones yesterday. They'll never forget it."

"Neither will I," I replied austerely.

"Reckon you won't." She smiled her slow smile. Then, as we emerged into the lobby, she remarked, "Kids really do say the darndest things. Like Sandy yesterday in Sunday school in The Marble Collegiate Church. The teacher asked if any of the kids could give an example of the commandment 'Love thy neighbor.' Sandy raised his hand and yelled, "I can! I can! Our neighbor, Mrs. Wood, loves her mouse and Peggy and me so much we all had breakfast together. The mouse ran around on the table and ate with us."

I pressed my lips tightly together. Mrs. Blackburn went on, "The teacher phoned to tell me about it. Oh, how we laughed! She told me to ask you to visit her class next Sunday—and oh, yes, to fetch your mouse."

"I will not," I said sharply. "I have my own church duties to attend to."

Looking snubbed, she went her way and I went mine. I grumbled under my breath, "One would think that mouse has a press agent."

As I took my afternoon walk around the outside of the tall iron fence that encloses Gramercy Park, I noticed small patches of dirty snow melting in the late-winter sunshine. Soon I overtook a set of parents, between them a leggy little girl, and as I passed I overheard her identify me: "That's the lady the mouse lives with."

I turned to glower back, but received such a broad grin from the father, such sunny smiles from the mother and the little girl, that I felt the wintry ice melt off my own face.

Nonetheless, I thought as I went rapidly on, this mouse affair is getting entirely out of hand. Walking faster and faster, I conducted a vigorous diatribe against the rodent. I computed the number of annoying changes and people it had brought into my life during the three months I had postponed getting rid of it. I told myself, "A sensible woman does not continue to let things happen to her. She takes some action."

And I would—I certainly would—before things went any further.

That evening when a knock sounded, I opened my inner door wondering who the intruder was this time. It was the children's father who grinned at me through the screen door. And he held something behind him in a manner disturbingly reminiscent of Father Lane concealing his mouse in its cage behind his back.

Mr. Blackburn spoke in the jovial, condescending tone one uses with children. "Bet you can't guess what gift I've brought to a lovely lady and her mouse."

In a veritable panic, I recalled his earlier statement, "You ought to have a pair." I closed my eyes. Oh, no! No! Another mouse shall never, never enter this apartment. I will refuse it with invincible firmness.

"Look!" he cried gaily.

When I dared to, he had brought out a bunch of long-stemmed red roses. Was it from relief, or because it was so many years since a man had brought me flowers, that tears filled my eyes? I unhooked and opened the screen door and accepted the roses in silence. Then he spoke with exaggerated gallantry.

"These roses are a tribute to your wonderful sense of justice. You see, my wife told me why you use that strong scent. And I must say, in this day and age when the rights of human beings are so often denied—by heaven, it sure is reassuring to meet a lady who recognizes the right of a mouse to smell something it likes —such as new-mown hay."

He considers me a maudlin, senile old idiot, I thought indignantly. I stood very erect. He handed me the evening paper. "It's raining, and I fetched it so you won't have to go out to the corner and get wet," he said and went whistling down the corridor.

I shut both my doors and leaned against the wall, weak in the knees from sheer relief. I looked across the room at Judith unconcernedly running on her wheel, and said, "I thought for one awful moment we were to have another mouse—a male—given to us whether we liked it or not."

"We"—"us," I had said. I had assumed that the Widow Judith would be as averse as I to the presence of another mouse—a male. As I put the roses in water, I wondered if I had the right to speak for her. In some disquiet, I asked myself, "Is the black mouse lonely?" And promptly I answered myself, in a peppery tone, "If so, it's just too bad, for there's nothing I can or will do about it. A male mouse will never cross the doorstep except over my dead body." And that, I thought, was that.

A day or so later, when I answered a knock at the door, there was Sandy outside, both hands behind *his* back.

"What have you got there?" I demanded suspiciously.

"Our dessert—tutti-frutti ice cream," he replied, with a happy grin. "I've come to have dinner with your mouse and you." He bolted to the kitchenette and opened its folding doors. "I'll put it in your refrig."

I felt no need of company. "I'm not having a very good dinner," I said. That made him pause.

"What are you having?"

I searched my memory for food I had heard mothers say their children wouldn't touch. "Hash," I improvised, "and spinach."

"O.K.!" he said cheerily. "I eat hash and I love spinach."

"I have only enough for one," I said shortly.

Slowly he retrieved his ice cream and went out, looking crestfallen.

One evening, when it was warm enough to have my casement windows wide open, I answered a thumping on my screen door and admitted Peggy, her arms overflowing with pajamas, bathrobe, coat, hat, umbrella, and other articles. "I've come to live with your mouse and you," she announced.

"Is your mother aware of it?" I inquired icily.

"Yep, she told me to. Mom said," and Peggy imitated the honey tone of her mother's voice, " 'If you must be over there morning, noon, and night, take your clothes and live over there.' "

"If you live here," I warned, "you'll have to take care of the cage." I hoped this would discourage her. It did not. She dropped her loose luggage to the floor. "O.K.! I'll clean it now to show you I can."

I reflected that it might as well be cleaned in the evening, so under my direction Peggy filled the bathtub with hot, soapy water. She rolled up her sleeves in a businesslike way and enthusiastically went to work. Suds flecked her snub nose and her straight blond hair, water splashed in all directions, but I must say she gave the cage as good a scrubbing as it had ever had. Nonetheless, as a further deterrent to her joining my household, I said, "Now you must scrub up the bathroom."

"Yippee!" She reached for the can of cleanser, but I stopped her, thinking it was time to involve her mother. "You must first ask your mother's permission."

She tore out and returned in seconds, yelling, "I will *so* live here with Mrs. Wood and her mouse!" She was followed by her mother, a cigarette smoking in one hand.

Mrs. Blackburn gave me a meaningful glance. "I told Peggy it may not be convenient for you to have her live here," she said.

"It isn't," I said flatly, and gave Peggy a stern look. "Stop acting like a baby. Come to live here when I invite you."

Peggy stopped in mid-yell. "When will that be?"

"When the mouse is trained to the leash and I need you to walk her," I said.

Peggy wiped her eyes on her sleeve. "O.K.," she said. Grinning, she collected her possessions from the floor. As she went out with her mother, Mrs. Blackburn looked back smiling.

"I'm surprised *you* never adopted any children," she said. "You certainly have an accommodating way with them."

If I had, it was something I had not known about myself. I placed the immaculate cage on the sill. But, I thought, it is useless for that indolent mother to butter me up. I will not relieve her of any of the care of her children. She had adopted them—they were her problem. And I still intended to maintain my privacy. "Or to regain it," I muttered, tight-lipped.

I frowned down at the Widow Judith. Neither had I known I could accommodate myself to a mouse, I thought wryly. Then I stiffened my backbone. I *must* take steps to rid myself of this magnet that drew such a miscellany of unwelcome people through my doorway.

It was about this time that I began to be haunted by faces: Peggy's, looking tear-stained as she picked up her luggage; Sandy's, looking crestfallen as he retrieved his ice cream; Mrs. Blackburn's looking rejected, Gentle Julia's looking wounded, Mr. Gardiner's looking rebuffed, Gladys's looking hurt. Their faces hung in my memory like tragic masks.

So on Saturday evening I hurried up to the Park Avenue church to confession. Eagerly I went down into the simple basement chapel where confessions are heard. But the tiny green light on Father Lane's cubicle, denoting a priest was inside, was not lit. So I knew Father Lane was late as usual. With a resigned sigh I knelt in a pew and thought peevishly, Why on earth does Father try to do more good deeds in one day than the law of time allows, and get behind with his duties? After a while he came running down the steps from the rectory, sprinted down the aisle and slid into a genuflection at home base—his confessional. His black cassock whisked inside and the green light came on.

Hastily I murmured the preparatory Confiteor and

fervently thanked God that when I entered the sanctity of the confessional, there at least I could be certain of discussing my grave spiritual problems with Father Lane without sharing his attention with his mouse.

But hardly had I entered the shadowy cubicle, lowered to my creaking knees and murmured, "Bless me, Father, for I have sinned," than he made a hasty sign of the cross and whispered anxiously through the dividing screen, "Before we begin, I want to ask a favor. When you leave, will you go to the Third Avenue pet shop and buy a big bag of deodorant sand for me. It's urgent."

"But, Father, on Saturdays the pet shop is closed."

In the dim light Father Lane's good face looked harassed. He held his head in his hands for a moment, then said, "Well, I suppose there's nothing to be done."

After that, I made only a routine confession; I had lost all desire to discuss the state of my soul and being for which I held mice responsible.

As I came out of the lower church, I felt that I was still dragging my troubles with me and I had no inclination to add Father Lane's predicament to them. "It's his problem, not mine," I argued. Yet I felt responsible, for I had delivered his mouse to him, I had thought in some malice, Let him find out what "the companionship of one of God's little creatures" entails. But I could not so easily shrug off Father's trouble, for now his harassed face was added to all the other tragic masks that haunted me.

That night, I slept fitfully, and had a horrendous nightmare. In it, I found myself seated amid a great congregation in an enormous cathedral. The altar was aglow with all its candles lit, as is usual for a solemn High Mass. The organ pealed forth. The choirboys entered in procession, led by an altar boy swinging a censer, but it did not hold the usual incense. No, the censer was sprinkling sand. Behind, came an altar boy holding aloft a crucifix, flanked by two boys holding flickering candles. Bringing up the rear, two pompous deacons escorted Father Lane between them, attired in magnificent vestments. He alone ascended to the altar. Then the whole congregation rose up and shouted, "Go away! You smell of mice!"

I woke in horror and black darkness. Had I been wakened by my own shouting or by the shouts of the 5 A.M. garbage collectors in the street below? I got up and switched on the light. My mouse trotted tirelessly on her wheel. I dressed, put a generous amount of deodorant sand into a shoe box, wrapped it in brown paper, and went out into the murky pre-dawn.

Before daylight, I was on upper Park Avenue, a solitary shadowy figure knocking at the rectory door. When a yawning night watchman opened up, I handed him my parcel, saying, "Take this to Father Lane at once." Then, in answer to his startled question, I said sharply, "Yes, wake him up. I'm awake, aren't I?"

Afterward as I climbed the stone steps into the church for the first Mass, soft gray daylight was flowing over the city. It was getting light earlier these days. Surely winter was almost over and spring well on its way.

When I reached home, the Widow Judith had not hidden to sleep. She trotted upon her wheel with—or so it seemed to me—some unusual urgency. Did she, too, sense that spring was just around the corner? "Is spring the mating season for mice?" I asked myself uneasily as I hung up my coat. Perhaps it would be safer to keep her confined to her cage, and not let her run about so freely on the window sill. Yet what had I to worry about? I had never heard of other mice in the building. The exterminator saw to that. Mice in the plural were not even a remote possibility in my life.

Still I could not rid myself of an uneasiness that increased in ratio to the lengthening of the days and the warming of the weather. I reiterated my resolve to abolish the black mouse from my abode. I even again contemplated giving the rodent to Gentle Julia's voracious cat.

"But," I said to myself one morning when the sun had come out after a shower, "it does seem a pity not to let the Widow Judith enjoy just one more spring —but by herself."

Before noon my phone rang, and when I answered, Father Lane spoke in a hoarse wheeze. "I've caught a severe spring cold," he said. "It's settled in my lungs, and the doctor has ordered me into the infirmary."

"I'm sorry," I said with cold emphasis, for I knew what was coming, and to myself I said obdurately, "I won't, I won't, I won't do it."

Father Lane said in his wheedling tone, "There's no one in the rectory who has had your experience in taking care of a mouse, no one I'd trust to look after mine. So I know you'll have the goodness to come up and take Michael Monk-Mouse home with you and look after the little fellow until I get well. I'll delay going into the infirmary until you can get here."

eight

On the way up to the rectory, I felt as if I were being impelled by some great power that I was helpless against. I sensed that agitating forces, which had been lurking just below the horizon, were now edging across the rim of my life. With fatalistic calm, I entered the Park Avenue rectory and greeted Father Lane with icy courtesy, unfolded the wrapping paper I had brought, and held out my hands for the cage.

Before giving it to me, Father Lane held the cage up in front of his face and, in a hoarse voice, addressed his mouse. "Now, Michael, remember what was in that sermon of mine you sampled. Teach Aunt Mary—"

"Don't call me 'Aunt' to a mouse," I snapped. "And I doubt your rodent can teach me anything I haven't already learned about life with a mouse."

Father gave me an odd glance. "Perhaps what one could not accomplish, two can," he said laconically.

"Not if I keep them in separate cages, they can't," I replied.

Then Father Lane, coughing and blowing, went off toward the infirmary, and I started homeward with a mounting fear that mice in the plural were no longer a remote possibility. "It seems I am not in control of my own life any more," I mused. For hadn't I vowed there were no conceivable circumstances that could induce me to admit a male mouse onto my premises? Yet here I was, bringing him in myself! Well, if Gentle Julia was in the elevator when I went up, I'd hand him over to her for cat food—so help me, I would.

But she was not in the elevator, and it occurred to me that I had not seen her since the evening she had discovered my cat was a mouse. She hadn't returned the book she had borrowed—one of a set, too. My ill-humor now turned against her. "She's a borrower—not a returner," I decided sourly. Then another possibility suggested itself: perhaps she was still waiting for me to invite her—or perhaps she was sick, all alone with that thin cat. And I hadn't inquired.

I remembered that Gladys had said the vanishing years had stolen away my sociability. I hadn't seen Gladys, either, since the night she had come to dinner and shrieked that she'd never thought to see the day when I'd have any pet. "But a *mouse!*"

Now, as I entered my apartment with another mouse, one quick glance showed an apparently empty cage on the window sill. The black mouse, invisible, slept within the shredded paper. I set down the wrapped cage on the floor with an angry bang—then hoped it had not wakened either mouse in case they were asleep. As I removed my coat I went over in my mind the double disagreeable tasks that now confronted me: *two* cages to scrub every morning, *two* mice to feed. For under no conditions whatever would I admit the mouse Michael into the Widow Judith's cage—

I paused abruptly in hanging up my coat; a hopeful thought had struck me. I had never actually ascertained the sex of my mouse. Perhaps the Widow Judith belied her name. Father Lane had seemed certain enough of Michael's gender; possibly my stolid black mouse and Father's slim tan one were of the selfsame sex.

My spirits rose. Perhaps, after all, there was no need to scrub two cages daily, but only one as usual, and to feed two mice in one cage was no more trouble than to feed one. "Two can live cheaper than one," I sang merrily.

But as I unwrapped Michael's smaller cage, a new worry assailed me. Even if both were males, they might contend for supremacy in the one domicile; one might exterminate the other. Since my ignorance of mice habits was abysmal, I decided I'd better proceed with extreme caution. I placed the small cage on the sill at a good safe distance from the large one.

There was an instantaneous reaction.

The Widow Judith, with one bound, came out of a deep sleep and the shredded paper. Michael leaped to the bars of his cage. In each mouse residence there ensued the wildest excitement—a sort of electrification. The stolid black mouse ran up and down the length of her cage with an agility she had never before displayed. The slim tan mouse, like a dapper dancing master, fleet-footed it around and around in his cage. Each tried the utmost to get at the other.

"But for the life of me," I puzzled, "I can't tell whether all this hoopla is caused by two males challenging each other to mortal combat or by the wilder music and stronger wine of love at first sight in the springtime—"

In uncertainty I watched them. Only one thing seemed clear: to put those two small dynamos into the same cage was extremely hazardous. If they were two males and fought it out to establish who was boss, the bigger black mouse surely would put an end to the slim tan one. Then what would Father Lane say?

"On the other hand," I reasoned, "if Judith is a female, and Michael is a devil-may-care young mouse —I'll be faced with the inevitable consequences."

Finally, I decided to chance it—oh, who knows why? —and to find out if it was indeed love or the hate of two competitive males. But I couldn't tell even after I admitted the tan mouse into the black mouse's cage. There followed a furious running about, a squeaking, a whirling of two small combative bodies. Then Michael retreated to a discreet distance, looking so oddly nonplussed and defeated that I felt a reluctant pity for him. "Really, Judith," I reproved, "widow or not, you're very inhospitable."

I stood contemplating them. The black mouse—larger, thicker—appeared more than ever a peasant type. The tan mouse—slimmer, prettier—was much more aristocratic. Maybe class difference prevented them from becoming friends. I was now positive both were males.

Michael made new overtures. He had more character than I'd given him credit for; the first qualification for success is, after all, a refusal to recognize defeat. Again there was a wild skirmish accompanied by angry squeaks. Again Michael retreated to a far corner, looking rejected and puzzled.

"Indubitably both *are* males," I assured myself, and in immense relief I settled down to my writing.

All day in the cage there was warfare, with offensive and defensive commotion. The tan mouse, though aggressive, seemed less bellicose than the black one, who seemed combative and affronted. "Perhaps she, too, objects to having her privacy invaded," I murmured once, with understanding. Possibly I ought to return Michael to his own cage. Then I starched my spine. "Darned if I'll clean two cages every morning. Let them fight it out."

By the time I was ready for bed, the skirmishes were so frequent, so deadly, that I racked my brains for some way to bring about peace. An idea occurred to me. With warring humans, there was nothing like a common peril to bring the contending factions together. Outside my windows, departing winter was lashing up a final storm, whipping sleet against the panes. So, instead of following my usual procedure of removing the cage to the coffee table at night, I left it where it was and opened wide two of the casement windows to admit the icy wind.

"There, you two!" I said. "Freeze or snuggle. Suit yourselves."

The next morning, when, shivering, I closed the windows, the two mice were sleeping soundly, sleek tan head snuggled on broad black back. They hadn't even bothered to crawl into the shredded paper. Probably utterly exhausted from battle, I thought. Looking down at them, I said softly, "There's a pleasant picture of brotherly love."

But I soon realized that their love was not brotherly. Dismayed but amused, I said, "So, Judith, you showed Michael that even though he's Park Avenue and a good catch, you were not a mouse of easy virtue. And you, Michael," I frowned down at the tan mouse, "Judith made you respect her as a *proper mouse,* eh?"

Then I sighed in resignation. "Well, all joy to you both."

Indeed, they did seem extraordinarily happy. After

the morning meal of sunflower seeds and a quaffing of rich milk, neither mouse hid away to sleep all day as was usual. Instead, they leaped upon the wheel and side by side ran merrily, merrily, as much as to sing, "Oh, oh, who wants to waste time in sleep when it is spring, tra-la, and we are young and in love and life is so exciting—so wonderful!"

Poignant regret stirred in my heart. Things long forgotten and wilted revived and rustled in my mind. Aging would be so much easier, I mused, if it went on only in autumn and one could be young again every spring. But, even as matters stood, my spirits rose in an unprecedented way. I felt a joyousness I had not experienced in many a long year. And I was glad I had not met Gentle Julia on the elevator the day before and given her the tan mouse for cat food. Gentle Julia—! I'd better find out why I had not seen her for so long.

When I dialled her phone number, she answered in a vague tone. I inquired about her health, and she said that she had been under the weather but would be better now. "Because you have phoned, and I thought nobody cared."

I felt the oblique accusation in her self-pity, but it did not douse my high spirits. With an unaccustomed urge to share, I said, "Come up. I want to show you something."

"Another cat?"

"Come and see."

When she came in, I noticed that her clothes were more rumpled than usual, as if she had slept in them night and day. She stared at the cage. "You've actually got a mate for the Widow Judith! I can hardly believe it. I could have sworn you would never take pity on the loneliness of a mouse."

I resented her thinking that I was stonyhearted, but I felt I should tell her the truth. "I did not bring the male mouse here out of pity for my mouse." I told her about Father Lane and his chest cold. "I couldn't very well refuse him, could I?" I asked irritably. "And I was ignorant of the sex of my mouse. I thought—I hoped—they were both of the same sex."

"Am I glad they weren't!" she cried rapturously. "I think things turned out wonderfully like this because of fate and spring."

"Spring may have something to do with it," I admitted. "And I confess to surprise at the chain of events that nature, or something, arranged so that two mice of the proper sex could get together to produce more mice. First Father Lane caught cold germs so I had to bring his mouse home; then you were not on the elevator so I could give the mouse to you to feed to your cat. Yet," I lifted skeptical eyebrows, "—the mating of two mice seems a trifling incident for fate to bother with."

Gentle Julia ignored my irony. "I'm sure it was fate that kept me dead drunk in my apartment so I couldn't be on the elevator," she declared.

The words "dead drunk" shocked me immeasurably. She saw this and said defensively, "Oh, I'm not afraid of the truth." But her eyes avoided mine, and I thought sadly, When courage fails, pride fails.

Watching the mice, she said warmly, "I'm so glad you weren't able to prevent all this springtime happiness and—"

"And the inevitable consequences," I finished in a glum voice.

"When will they arrive?"

"How on earth should I know?"

"Well, it won't be nine months," she warned. She added, "I'm returning your book." She did indeed have the missing volume of *The Arabian Nights*. As she replaced it among the others on the shelves, she asked, "May I borrow another book?"

"Take any one you like," I offered, and she selected Durant's *The Reformation*.

As she went out, she said shyly, "I'll be all right now—for a time." She could hardly lift her eyelids to look at me, and her green eyes were bleary. "Thanks for asking me up to share the nuptial joy of the mice. Any time you want to come down to see me and my cat—but, of couse, *you're* never lonely. You're one of those strong, self-sufficient characters."

She departed.

The way she had said "strong, self-sufficient characters"—as if such residents on this earth required Christian forbearance from those who were more human —annoyed me only momentarily. The unpleasant flavor she had left on the day evaporated, and with a resurgence of my former expansive mood I phoned Gladys.

She was astonished. "I say!" she cried. "What has happened to you?"

"What makes you think something has?"

"Because you're never the one to phone—I am. So something must have happened to you. Are you getting married, by any chance?"

"No, but Judith should be."

"You got a mate for her! Oh, I say! I never thought I'd live to see the day when you would have *two* mice."

"You'll live to see the day when I have a cageful," I retorted, "if *I* live to see it. No doubt I will. I've survived sharing life with two mice, and doubtless my stamina will be equal to myriads."

Silence on the phone. Then Gladys said, "You not only sound human, you sound positively gay. I'll come over this afternoon for a spot of tea. I'll bring—"

"Don't bring anything," I cut in.

"You thought I was going to say I'd bring Armstrong-Jones," she said, and laughed. "You haven't mellowed enough to endure my parakeet. But if I can put up with your mice, you ought to put up with my bird. However, what I was about to say was I'll bring some English raisin bread for tea."

While we were having our tea, there came a pounding on my door, and I explained, "It's two neighbor children." But when I opened the door, not only Sandy and Peggy but two others peered up at me with eager, expectant faces. They were identical twin boys, so blond they looked bleached, and they were audibly sucking lollipops.

"They wanna see your mouse," Sandy said, and

Peggy cried, "They've just moved in, though the grouchy woman tried to keep them out. She hates kids!"

"Why must children always scream so?" I asked in annoyance, and Sandy replied, "Because if we don't, grownups pay no attention to what we want."

"Humph," I said and let them in. The four children ran to the cage. One twin looked up at me from under white cotton lashes with eyes bright as mica disks. "Poke the mouse out so we can see it. Please poke it out."

Obligingly I poked with a pencil. Out crawled the black mouse and out crawled the tan mouse.

"Two!" cried the twins. "Hurray!"

"A pair!" shouted Sandy. "Whoopee!"

"Now you'll get baby mice," yelled Peggy. "Yippee!"

"Hurray, whoopee, and yippee," I said calmly.

Then Sandy tugged at his forelock worriedly. "You better not let the grouchy woman know you've got a pair. She hates kids, so she'll sure hate mice."

"It's a thought to keep in mind," I replied. "Now my guest and I wish to finish our tea, so please take your departure."

As they passed the tea tray, four pairs of eyes went to the raisin bread. Gladys rose to the occasion. Each child left with a large slice.

At the door, Peggy turned and said, "Now we'll have to come in morning, noon, and night to watch out for the baby mice."

"So you better leave your inside door unlocked and the screen door unhooked," advised Sandy. "Then us kids can get in and out without so much bother to us."

"It's a thought," I said grimly.

When I returned to the tea table, Gladys eyed me in speculation. "It's a thought all right, but will you accept it?"

"The easily opened doors would save *me* a lot of bother as well as the children," I said evasively.

"The easily opened doors also might be dangerous to you and your possessions, what with all the sneak thieves about these days and the attacks on lone women."

"Oh, *I'm* not one of those emotionally starved females who look under their beds before retiring," I said. "Nor one to cower in my apartment in fear of male intruders."

Gladys looked cynical. "Then why the *two* doors?"

"It should be obvious the screen door is for ventilation," I replied as I poured myself a cup of tea.

"It should be obvious that leaving your two doors unlocked might remove the final barriers between you and the world." Her eyes searched my face. "What about your well-guarded privacy? Aren't you afraid you will lose all control of your life?"

"Humph! The control of my life has already been taken over by mice." I gave a staccato laugh.

"Great day!" Gladys stared at me in surprise. "I never thought to live to see the day when you would laugh at yourself."

"If you haven't learned to laugh at yourself by the time you're my age," I replied, "you never will."

nine

One day, Father Lane phoned and said, in his normal, cheery voice, "My cold is much better, but I'm still in the infirmary. How's Michael Monk-Mouse?"

"Monk-Mouse, my eye!" I exclaimed. "I've news for you, Father. Michael isn't a church mouse. He went courting. The Widow Judith succumbed to his charms, and now Michael is growing a mustache and strutting about because he's going to become a father."

Father Lane chuckled. "I'd hoped for some such eventuality. Well, keep me informed."

I should have informed myself—read up on mice and their habits—but I didn't. I just took things as they came—even mice. As the days lengthened, Judith grew plumper and plumper. Even the children noticed it. One morning, Peggy, Sandy, and the bleached twins were at the window sill; all casements were flung wide open, for spring had taken a firm foothold on the weather. Sandy looked at the cumbersome black mouse climbing onto the wheel and commented, "It'll be any day now."

"It looks like it," I replied, quailing.

That afternoon, Gladys phoned to say a producer who once had directed her in "Mrs. Warren's Profession" had given her passes to a play, and she wondered if I would go with her that evening. I said I would, and after a quick dinner I dressed for the theatre, put on my hat, and was ready to leave when I heard tiny squeaks in the cage.

Hurrying to the cage, I saw Judith fussing about among a lot of revolting pink worms. Nobody would have recognized them as baby mice except their mother. She seemed satisfied with them, and looked smug, matronly, and occupied. Michael had retreated to a far corner, as abashed as any new father with his nose put out of joint, knowing he is expected to keep out from underfoot at that crucial time.

I took a quick glance at the clock, laid down my

purse and got some scissors, and hastily cut blue and pink tissue paper into shreds. "Blue for boys, pink for girls," I said. "It stands to reason there'll be some of both." I made a nest and thrust it into the cage, saying, "Here, Mother Mouse, is your bassinet."

She inspected it and made a few adjustments, then carried the pink worms into it, one by one. I counted nine and groaned. Now I had eleven mice. "And you are responsible," I accused Michael.

He ignored me. Indeed, he ignored the nest within which Judith and her progeny were now concealed. He kept his proper distance and sat unconcernedly munching dry oatmeal. If he felt left out in the cold, no one was going to know he cared. Again I looked at the clock. Botheration! I was going to be late. I picked up my purse and gloves and rushed out.

Down in the lobby, I hastened past Gentle Julia coming in with her orange cat in her arms, said facetiously, "Michael is passing out the cigars," and she called after me, "Did you remove him from the cage?"

"What for?" I inquired over my shoulder. "Let him do his share of taking care of his children," and she made a scandalized face.

Outside, as I waited for a bus, I thought in annoyance, Why was she looking so horrified? What have I done *now* to earn her disapproval? These sensitive females—showing all their feelings on their faces! I chided. Then my bus arrived and I forgot her.

In the darkened theatre, as I settled down into my seat beside Gladys, she whispered, "Why so late?" I whispered back the reason, and at once she asked,

"Where is Michael?" I replied *sotto voce,* "He was hovering about looking as superfluous as any new father. Why do you ask?"

"Shh!" somebody said behind us.

It was a good play, though possibly I thought so because I hadn't seen one for so long. Afterward I took Gladys into a drugstore for some refreshment, and since we were preoccupied with discussing the play, neither of us mentioned mice until we parted. Then, as she climbed on her crosstown bus, she spoke down to me. "I say! Let me know if a Greek tragedy has occurred in the mouse cage." The bus started, we said a hasty goodbye and as I crossed Broadway to catch a downtown bus, I murmured, "How theatrical Gladys is! What tragedy could possibly befall baby mice in a cage?"

At midnight, when I switched on my living-room light and looked into the cage, I looked upon carnage. The pink and blue tissue-paper nest was bespattered with blood. I saw five tiny beheaded pink bodies. "Oh, no, no!" I cried, in horror.

But Judith was moving about, calmly accepting the inevitability of some tragedy in a lifetime. And Michael—Michael ran lightheartedly on the wheel. I glared at him, opened the cage, and grabbed his tail and flung him angrily into his own small cage. I slammed down its gate.

"There! You odious little cannibal."

Then, grim-lipped, with my hat still on, I set about cleaning up the cage and removing all traces of Michael's slaughter of the innocents. Mastering my squeamishness, I scooped out the mangled remains of five infinitesimal baby mice one by one in a demitasse spoon. I thought with guilt, I am an accessory to Michael's crime. Ignorance of mouse common law was no excuse. I certainly should have read up on mice.

Feeling sad and sick at heart, I disposed of the five corpses in the bathroom. "This, then, is the end of all that joy in the spring, tra-la," I said bitterly. But perhaps not. Possibly some lives could yet be saved.

Fashioning a fresh bassinet of pink and blue tissue paper, I put it in the cage, carefully spooned the four survivors into it, and said sadly, " 'And then there were four.' " They didn't look too well, but they were whole and they breathed. Judith accepted what was left to her and made the best of it. She pulled the shredded paper over herself and her four remaining infants, and all was still.

I sighed deeply. Wearily I took off my hat, undressed, and crawled into my bed without removing its spread. But I could not sleep. I had a sense of irreparable loss. "Don't be such a fool. They were only mice," I whispered. "The little pests we pay exterminators to do away with." Yet I could not rid myself of the sense that I had been accessory to the crime of infanticide.

The next morning while I was still in my hair rollers and housecoat, gulping down black coffee to get me going, there was a knock. I had prudently locked my doors for the night. When I opened them, Gentle Julia entered softly in her furred slippers and bathrobe. She spoke in a hushed tone that told me she knew what to expect. "I came to inquire about the baby mice."

"Michael killed five," I reported drearily, and then demanded, "Last night when I saw you, why didn't you tell me to take him out of the cage?"

Embarrassed, she avoided my glance. "Well, leaving him in the cage could have been an easy way for you to be rid of the nuisance of baby mice."

"You thought me capable of deliberately placing helpless little beings in jeopardy?" I cried indignantly.

She did not remind me that I had once deliberately contemplated feeding the parent mice to her cat. "I see that you feel dreadful," she said sympathetically, but she looked pleased. "You look awful, and I didn't know strong characters could."

"Loss of sleep plays hob with us older women," I conceded. "But this black coffee will revive me. Sit down and have a cup with me."

She gazed at me in a new way as I poured it, and I thought uncomfortably, She thinks that I, too, need a stiff drink now and then to endure life. She drank her coffee standing. "I mustn't stay. I want to slip down the back stairs again before the building is astir. I'd die of mortification if any man saw me in these curlers and wearing this old red bathrobe."

On the way out, she said, "Thanks for sharing your tragedy with me—and your brand of strong drink."

As I shut my door, the phone rang. It was Gladys. "Well?" she asked, and I said indignantly, "You know well enough, and why didn't you warn me last night when I came to the theatre that I ought to hurry home and remove Michael from the cage? A fine friend you are. And—"

"Whoa! Hold your horses," she cut in. "I knew it was too late—that murder had been done. Did he devour them all?"

I said four might survive with care, and added in a peppery tone. "So if you have any more knowledge of mice that I ought to have, for heaven's sake, tell me."

"My knowledge of mice is negligible," she admitted. "But I don't imagine there's anything more you need to find out—or that you can do."

Any more damage I can do, she means, I thought bitterly. Aloud I said, "Except to keep the cage clean and antiseptic—I'm sure that's important."

"I'm sure it's important to you," she replied dryly.

At noon, Sandy, Peggy, and the twins came in. The minute they saw Michael in solitary (he had emerged to drink milk), Peggy cried, "The baby mice have come!"

"How do you know?" I demanded.

"Because you've put the father mouse out of the cage so he can't eat his children," Sandy replied. It seemed that even children knew that much about mice. The four stared, big-eyed, at the bassinet of colored tissue paper. Peggy told the twins, "There are nine baby mice in there."

"How do you know?" I inquired, taken aback.

Sandy replied, "Because that's how many a mouse mother usually has—my dad says."

"A mouse *might* have fewer," I suggested, and hoped fervently that eventually there would be four whole little mice to show the children.

So every morning I cleaned the home cage meticulously, determined to keep the nursery antiseptic. Carefully I would remove the tissue-paper nest, spoon out the four survivors into a freshly made nest, and return it to the cage. Judith would hover about uneasily, but she had to put up with my ideas of hygiene. With her customary wise acquiescence to the way of life, she accepted me as another of its hazards.

One evening, as I sat sewing, I heard a swishing in the home cage. I surmised that Judith had emerged to take her exercise on the wheel; perhaps it needed oiling. I went on sewing, but the swishing began to sound ominous. I glanced up—and made a wild leap to the rescue.

For the pink and blue tissue paper had become entangled in the wheel spokes and was furiously slapping around and around. The bassinet—oh, my heavens! With the four baby mice in it! When I succeeded in disentangling the tissue paper, three more tiny mice lay motionless. Sick at heart, I spooned them out and disposed of them like their siblings before them. When I returned, Judith, seemingly unperturbed, was exercising on the wheel.

"*You* allow nothing to interfere with *your* habits," I accused her. I picked up the sole surviving baby mouse on my silver spoon. " 'And then there was one.' " It seemed vigorous. "It would have to be," I said grimly, "to have survived that joy ride."

Scrutinizing it closely, I discovered that it no longer

resembled a pink worm; its skin was dark gray and wrinkled, like that of an infinitesimal rhinoceros. Its minute ears were mere marks, its eyes dots. But it actually looked like a tiny mouse. "It truly is a mouse, tail and all," I marvelled. How could a pink worm have become a little mouse in the course of only a few days?

I placed the infant in the tissue-paper bassinet and put it carefully into a far corner of the cage. Then I set about figuring out a sure method to keep the wheel from being turned. I fetched a length of hemp cord and wound it in and out, in and out, through the wheel in a most intricate way, knotting it as a sailor once had taught me in my youth. Finally, I tied the ends of the cord to the top of the cage.

"There!" I said triumphantly. "I have coped with the mouse instinct to run, run, run." Highly pleased with myself I went to bed.

The next morning when I awakened, I sat up, uttered an anguished cry, and leaped from bed to cage in one bound. Judith was serenely trotting on the turning wheel, the tissue-paper bassinet again entangled and swishing merrily around and around. One glance showed the hemp cord neatly coiled beneath the wheel, as if saved for some possible future need. It had been skillfully gnawed where gnawing was most effective.

"Oh, Judith," I wailed, *"must* you take your exercise, come disaster, come death!"

I disentangled the bassinet and searched out the last baby mouse. It lived, but not enthusiastically.

Judith hopped off the wheel, turned her back on me and her winded infant, stretched lazily, and crawled into the nest alone to sleep.

"Don't you care—don't you care at all?" I cried.

I spooned up the tiny listless mouse. I breathed on it until it stirred and revived. Very carefully, I placed it in the tissue-paper nest close to Judith.

She kicked it out.

Again I placed it near her. She made an impatient movement that plainly said, "Why can't you see that that thing is finished as a mouse if I can?" And she kicked it out again. Not knowing what else to do, I lifted the limp mouse onto a bit of cotton, placed it in the corner of the cage, and tucked it in.

Then I went to the kitchenette to make coffee, wishing I had something stronger. Perhaps I could borrow something from Gentle Julia—but, no, better not.

I refrained from looking into the cage again until after I had dressed, scrubbed Michael's bachelor quarters, and returned it to the window sill. Finally, with quaking heart, I approached the home cage. Then I, too, knew the thing on the cotton was finished as a mouse. Unconcernedly, Judith again trotted on her wheel. Her whole attitude seemed to say philosophically, "Well, life must go on as usual, you know."

"You certainly take your bereavement lightly," I chided. I looked from her to Michael. He munched sunflower seeds. "You two!" I exclaimed, appalled at the cold finality of nature as manifested in mice.

That day, Gentle Julia came up to return the book she had borrowed. When I told her about the demise of the last infant mouse, she observed softly, "Nature confers death very carelessly—and lavishly, doesn't it?" Then she added eagerly, "But nature also bestows life very abundantly—especially to mice. Just give Judith and Michael another chance."

"Never!" I cried as dramatically as Gladys could have done. I cast a baleful glance at Michael. "He doesn't deserve it. It's horrible the way male mice destroy their own progeny."

"Not only mice," Gentle Julia said, replacing the book on the shelf. "Durant says that in the sixteenth century the Sultan Suleiman destroyed all his progeny—sons, grandsons, and great-grandsons—to get rid of interlopers and possible claimants to his throne."

"Men!" I exclaimed. "Mice!"

I dreaded telling the children of the catastrophe and cast about in my mind for an easy way to do it. Finally, I tied a scarf of black crêpe to the home cage. When Sandy and Peggy came in, all they needed was one look.

"You drowned them," Peggy accused.

"I did not," I denied sharply. "What do you think I am?" She didn't say but she looked it through the slit in her bangs.

Sandy said soberly, "Michael killed them before you put him out of the cage."

I did not reply at once, struggling with my conscience. It would not permit me to shift all the blame onto a mouse. Surely I ought to be big enough to shoulder my share. "Michael killed five. I killed four," I admitted.

"How?" demanded Peggy.

"With kindness," I replied sadly.

Peggy put her moist, dirty little hand in mine. "O.K.," she said, with an acceptance of life as it is that equalled Judith's.

There remained the unpleasant further necessity of telling Father Lane about the tragedy in the world of mice. I dreaded that ordeal.

ten

I postponed telling Father Lane as long as I could. He can't possibly blame me, I argued inwardly—not when I tell him of the care I took to give Judith the benefit of my human knowledge of hygiene. While I was still trying to vindicate myself to myself, Father Lane phoned me. "Well?" he asked tentatively.

I launched into explanations, giving him the execrable details. Defensively I ended, "The wholesale death of those little mice certainly was not due to any culpable negligence of mine."

"It certainly wasn't," he replied caustically, and added, "I hope now you've learned your lesson, and in future you'll know enough not to interfere with nature and God-given animal instincts."

"Such as your Michael's instinct to do away with interlopers by beheading his own progeny," I retorted.

Father Lane ignored my sarcasm. "Perhaps next time you'll use the good sense God gave you and leave matters to the mother mouse, who knows her own business better than you do."

"There isn't going to be a next time," I said in a brittle tone. "There isn't anything in this wide world that could induce me to repeat what I've just been through. I feel drained." Then, deviously, I inquired, "When will you get out of the infirmary?" And he replied in a breezy voice, "Oh, I'm out."

But he had understood the reason for my question, because he added quickly, "I haven't yet regained my strength and I must curtail my activities for a time, so I know you will be kind enough to keep Michael a while longer."

"In his *own* cage," I said emphatically.

"Poor Michael," Father commiserated, "and with spring in full bloom, too."

"Spring or no spring," I said sourly, "nature is not going to bloom again in my vicinity in the matter of mice." I hung up.

So Michael was restricted to his small bachelor

quarters and Judith had the big, roomy cage to herself and seemed to enjoy her privacy. But I paid the price of her uninvaded solitude; every morning I scrubbed two cages. I worked out a new system. I placed Michael's at one end of the table, Judith's at the other. First I'd let her out to run about freely while I tended to her domicile. She didn't even bother to visit Michael through the bars of his cage.

However, when she was again locked up, and I released Michael— Whiz! Like a shot, he was over at her cage bars, frantically trying to get in and join her, for his was a precipitant passion. For a time, she would ignore him, calmly munch sunflower seeds, or trot sedately on her wheel. Finally, with an air of "Oh, well, I might as well get this tiresome duty over with," she would amble over for a casual conversation with her liege lord through the bars of her cage. Ardently he would try to squeeze through to embrace her. Not for Michael the subtle, circuitous advance by way of a preliminary intellectual discussion of the libido. Oh, no. His was the direct, honest approach.

But I kept his love platonic.

Then came a sunny morning when soft breezes drifted in through the open casements. Both cages had been cleaned and placed at opposite ends of the table, with Michael shut up in his and Judith still at liberty. I turned away to accept a bunch of tulips Mr. Blackburn handed in when I answered his knock, and when I came back to the table, I was aghast to see that Michael had contrived to open his cage gate.

He and Judith ran about happily together. "But platonically, thank my lucky stars!" I exclaimed.

Quickly I grabbed them by their tails and tossed them into their separate cages. As I securely locked the gates, I was grateful that nothing untoward had had time to occur.

Before the lapse of many days, however, it became obvious that on that balmy sunny morning, while I looked the other way to accept the tulips, Michael had expressed himself. I phoned Father Lane and informed him that Judith was again *enceinte.* "Just imagine," I exclaimed in reluctant wonder, "in the split second while my back was turned, plenteous new beings were caused to begin life."

"So a miracle was worked while your back was turned and you couldn't prevent it, eh?" His voice brimmed with delight. "His will be done."

"It's easy for you to say that," I grumbled. "You don't have to put up with the disagreeable things involved in this second attempt to replenish the earth with mice."

"This time," he said sternly, "I hope you'll remember what I told you about minding your own business, and trust to your mouse's God-given maternal instinct."

"This time," I replied succinctly, "I certainly shall not trust to your Michael's God-given paternal instinct."

I hung up.

I addressed the black mouse. "This time when you are brought to childbed, to blazes with hygiene. I'll let your instinct rule the roost and we'll see what happens."

As I went about my duties, I reflected that I had

had a chance to recuperate between batches of mice and that I was really not too sorry that Michael had outwitted me. For one thing, I had felt no little compunction because my meddling, though well-meant, had brought his earlier attempt at fatherhood to naught. Too, I felt that Judith deserved another chance at the complete fulfillment of motherhood, which my ignorance had cheated her of before.

I badly needed some information about mice. I phoned Mrs. Blackburn and told her that Judith was pregnant again. "Is that so?" she asked abstractedly, and then said, "Oh, Mrs. Wood, we've just returned from the adoption agency with the new baby. You remember I told you we were going to adopt another one? I certainly have my hands full. Thank goodness for hot running water and the diaper service. Do you know anything about the care of a baby?"

Since she obviously did, her query could only mean that she had me in mind as a possible and convenient baby-sitter. I replied in a firm tone that I knew nothing at all about infants.

"Well, I'll tell the children Judith is expecting again," she said, "and now if you will excuse me—"

I excused her; I had lost all desire to discuss the prenatal care of an expectant mouse.

In a matter of seconds, Sandy and Peggy rushed in pell-mell. "We've got a new baby—yippee!" cried Peggy.

"It's a boy!" shouted Sandy. "Whoopee!"

They ran to the home cage and eyed plump Judith.

"Yes," said Peggy, "she's going to have more babies."

Sandy eyed me coldly. "How can she when you were mean and kept them apart?"

The children's acceptance of sex, its possibilities and limitations, always nonplussed me. Now I was also disconcerted by their summary judgment of me. I began lamely, "Well—it was like—"

"Like I told Dad, you aren't really mean—and like Dad said, you weakened because it's spring." Sandy nodded wisely. "My Dad and I sure knew."

"You did, did you?" I said irately, thinking that the father and his tulips were responsible for this new probability of more baby mice. Then I remembered that Mr. Blackburn, when a boy in Kentucky, had kept a pair of mice in the tobacco shed, and I said, "Ask your father to stop in this evening. I want his advice about something."

When Mr. Blackburn came in later, he was beaming. "I feel as happy as a dog that's treed a coon," he announced. "Have you seen the fine baby boy we have over at our place? No? Well, you must come right over. He's just waked up and is yelling bloody murder. He's got the lungs of a hog-caller."

He had. Sandy, Peggy, the parents, and I stood around the blue-trimmed bassinet looking down at the mite of squalling humanity. "He's adopted," Sandy informed me, "like Peggy and me."

When I expressed proper admiration for the ugly red-wrinkled infant, Mr. Blackburn laughed. "Oh, don't be so kind. You know it's scarcely recognizable as a human being. It's hard to believe that little screaming thing will ever be a man." Then, remembering, he glanced across the bassinet at me. "You wanted to talk to me about something?"

"I've forgotten what it was," I answered carelessly. It seemed neither the time nor the place to consult him about baby mice.

Back home, I phoned Peter and Jane, who had given me the black mouse at Christmas. I spoke in a knowledgeable tone. "Of course, I know a father mouse must be removed from the cage, and that a mother mouse's instincts would tell her all she needs to know—that is, if she were living in a natural wild state—but in a cage she may need my help."

"All you need to do, Mrs. Wood," Peter said, "is to put a cardboard box and bits of cotton in the cage. The mouse will do the rest."

I did not attend to it at once, for I had not noted the length of time of the first pregnancy, and I was certain it would take a long while to produce new beings—even mice.

However, in what seemed an astonishingly short number of days I heard familiar tiny squeaks in the cage, and once more I saw the dreadful pink worms. "Well, here we go again," I said, and went to fetch a cardboard carton I'd saved for the purpose. When I returned with it, I was amazed to see that Judith had risen from childbed and was trotting on the wheel. No gymnastics, mind you, just a cautious, slow trot, which reminded me of our human custom of getting a new mother up on her feet and walking as soon as possible.

Have animals instinctively known the wisdom of getting up and doing long before we humans learned it? I wondered.

I eyed the black mouse with new respect, feeling confident now that she did indeed know her own business. I put the carton and cotton bits into the cage, murmuring apologetically, "I'm sorry to be so late with these supplies, but I didn't realize you should have had them earlier to prepare for your blessed event. Now, fix your bassinet to suit yourself."

The sudden availability of things required to fill her urgent needs caused the imperturbable mother mouse no surprise. She calmly inspected the carton inside and out and accepted it as suitable. Busily, methodically, with nose and paws, she pushed the bits of cotton inside and then herself went in. The carton quivered and shook with the speed and energy of her manipulations as she made up for time lost by my negligence as a provider.

She emerged at last and carried her infants in, one by one. I counted nine. "Once more, I have eleven mice," I observed with satisfaction. From inside the carton, Judith pushed the cotton up against its open end, blocking my view.

She had shut the door in my face, as much as to say, "This time, you mind your own business and I'll mind mine."

eleven

For several days, I exercised admirable restraint and kept my hands off the cage. The deodorant sand kept it from becoming obnoxious, and though now and again I sniffed suspiciously through the bars, I could detect no disagreeable odor from the carton, either. Regularly, Judith emerged for her exercise and food. Regularly, I put in unusually large amounts of milk, oatmeal, and sunflower seeds.

"For now you must eat for ten," I would remind her, and I marvelled that such a small creature could indeed take in enough nourishment for herself and nine growing mice. I looked upon the black mouse with more and more respect, and she seemed to regard herself with equal esteem. There was something in the way she trotted out for food and ate it, the careful manner in which she took her daily exercise—a certain important air of discharging her duties—that seemed to express a smug, conscious motherhood.

Though her infants were out of my sight, they were more than ever in my mind. I told myself I could not indefinitely leave that cage unscrubbed and unreplenished with fresh sand. So one morning, after I had attended to Michael's bachelor quarters, I left his cage on one end of my table and placed Judith's on the other. Biting my lip, I looked at it and pondered.

Surely now it could be cleaned without unduly disturbing the next generation of mice. Carefully I lifted out the carton of little mice and placed it gently on the table. Judith came running to inspect her nursery. Did she remember my previous fussy interference and its tragic results? If so, she seemed satisfied that if I had done any harm now, it was negligible.

She began a leisurely jaunt about the table, ignoring the cage at the far end in which Michael, greatly agitated, was showing the utmost interest in her peregrinations. By now, I knew my mouse, her temperament and character, so I was not surprised at the cool indifference she showed her husband. She paused to select a sunflower seed, sat up and munched it slowly, then washed her face. Only after she had shown him how little importance he had in her life did she amble over for a calm reunion with the exuberant Michael.

If he was informed that again he was the father of nine and that there was now nothing he could do about it, he showed neither dismay nor joy in his parenthood. Michael was still the debonair mouse—still the ardent wooer. Judith, bored with such emphasis on the physical aspects of love, left him flat.

I attended to her cage, replaced the carton within it, and was soon engrossed in my memoirs.

Everyone who had known of Judith's earlier pregnancy and loss now knew that she had been safely delivered of a second litter of baby mice, all of whom were developing invisibly within the carton. A breeze of excited expectancy was blowing through our building, fanning out through Gramercy Park, uptown to the Jesuit rectory, westward to Gladys's brownstone.

Daily, Gladys phoned to inquire, "I say! Have they come out yet?" Every evening, Mr. Blackburn, on his way home from the bank where he worked, opened my screen door, poked in his head and the evening paper, and asked eagerly, "Well, how are things?"—meaning mice. Frequently, Mr. Gardiner waylaid me in the lobby to inquire past the toothpick in his mouth, "Any news?" And in the confessional Father Lane would murmur a questioning "Well?"

One day, Gentle Julia came in to ask, as usual,

"Have the sweet baby mice come out yet?" Then she stood looking down at the carton. "I have an old maid's curiosity," she said. "I wonder what's going on in there."

"The baffling mystery of all developing beings," I replied eruditely, then added, "Though possibly I'm treating the topic of growing mice with too much importance. These days, I may tend to see uniqueness in the commonplace and to forget the infinitesimal part mice occupy in the vast scheme of things."

"Every living thing, no matter how tiny, is unique, I always say," Gentle Julia said, in her purring voice. "And you can't treat men, mice, or cats as unimportant beings in the big scheme of things without being unfair to them and to yourself." Surprised, I was considering her philosophical pronouncement when she admitted, "I got that idea straight from the horse's mouth—though maybe Martin Buber mightn't like being called a horse."

I reflected that Gentle Julia's conversation, whatever else it might be, was never insipid. Though her appearance was unprepossessing and undeniably she was, like all parasites, ready to fasten upon anything, I felt a growing liking for her, despite her alcoholic aura. Her friendliness nowadays was always warm and reliable.

She borrowed another book; this time it was *The Phenomenon of Man* by Teilhard de Chardin. I made a note of it on a pad, and another in my mind that soon I'd be receiving back the philosophy of Father

Teilhard via the more understandable interpretation given it by Gentle Julia.

Hardly had she gone when Father Lane came in, brisk, breathless, and in a hurry, as usual. "I was just passing on my way to the Catholic Charities," he explained. "I'm late, but I had to drop in to see if the little mice have come out yet to liven up your solitude."

"They have not," I replied crisply, "but my solitude is considerably livened up by callers who come in to inquire about the mice. You're the second one this morning. Sit down, Father."

"Thanks, but I can't linger. Who was the first?"

"Miss Tate, who lives with a cat. She brought to my attention the right attitude to take toward mice and men—an attitude that seems to me to upset the proper balance of things."

"If," he said, assuming his sacerdotal tone, "she brought to your attention that you're responsible to God for your attitude toward all His creation, I can't see why this upsets your sense of the balance of things."

"It upsets my sense of my own importance," I replied aggrievedly. "I have less and less time to write. I seem to live only for the increase of mice. Sometimes I visualize myself as mouse-size in importance and Judith as life-size."

"Excellent!" Father Lane said, his blue eyes disappearing in crinkles under his bushy brows. "That will teach you humility."

I bridled. "It seems that everybody can philosophize about mice and me—everybody who has not the troublesome care of them."

"Have you any idea when they will come out?" he asked, going toward the door.

"Not the slightest," I replied as I held the door open for him. He called back from the elevator, "Well, keep me informed."

My next visitors that morning were Sandy and Peggy. They burst in to stare round-eyed at the carton. Peggy jumped up and down in excitement. "I just can't wait till they come out!" she cried. "Oh, when do you think they will?"

I let out a long sigh. "I wish to heaven I knew."

Each morning I lifted out the carton, I noted that it became heavier and heavier. One morning, it was so heavy that I grew anxious. "The growing mice must be crowding the nursery to its gunwales," I murmured. What if they should smother! Later that day, I perceived that Judith, too, recognized the danger, for she pushed a goodly portion of cotton out of the carton to make more room for her growing children.

The next morning when I lifted out the heavy carton I could no longer restrain my curiosity. I pushed aside the remaining cotton and peeked inside. The interior was stuffed to capacity with wriggling, furry little mice. They would certainly suffocate unless I did something about it. By now they must be robust enough for me to help them with no risk to their lives.

I searched through closets and found a larger carton. I put in fresh cotton, then took up the old nursery, placed its open end within the larger carton, and, holding my breath, shook the unseen little mice from the old nursery into the new one. There were surprised squeaks—thumps. I counted thumps—one, two, three, four, five—then I lost count. My heart contracted, for it had seemed as if there were fewer than nine. "Oh, dear!" I exclaimed, dismayed. "Has *she* lost some of this batch?"

Worriedly I placed the new nursery inside the cage. Judith hurried into it to ascertain the safety of her offspring. While she inspected the new nursery, I inspected the old one.

Gingerly, with tweezers, I extracted the remaining cotton, expecting to find two or three lifeless mice. Nary a corpse. Had a mother mouse ways of disposing of dead bodies? For it didn't seem possible that all nine had survived. I sniffed at the cotton. It seemed as sweet as new-mown hay. Now, how in heaven's name, I wondered, was it possible for a mother mouse, with no hot running water and no diaper service, to keep nine baby mice and herself antiseptically clean?

Next morning when I peeked into the new nursery, a multitude of rumps and tails met my gaze, for the little mice had turned their backs to me—or to the light. They wriggled and shoved on top of one another, trying to hide. I counted rumps. There were nine, all right.

Gazing at them, I felt a pang of jealousy at the

fecundity of Judith—and also a sense of inferiority to this mouse in another matter. I was chagrined that because of my ignorance Michael had beheaded five of the first litter, and because of my finicky care four more had met untimely death. "While now," I muttered, scowling, "under Judith's instinctive care all nine have survived."

I replaced the nursery in the cage and went to phone Father Lane. I told him there were nine. "And just think," I said, in an awed voice, "Judith has saved every last one of them! Six are black like their mother. Three are golden tan, so your Michael cannot deny their parentage. Those three are the spit and image of him."

"You don't say!" Father Lane sounded immensely pleased. "When do you suppose they'll come out?"

"I'll let you know the minute they do," I assured him. "I've promised the children a coming-out party for mice. I'll send you an engraved invitation."

"I'll come," he promised with alacrity. "And I'll bring as many altar boys as I can round up."

That afternoon, however, my heart sank when an imperative knock sounded and I looked through my screen door and saw a policeman standing outside. The thought flashed through my mind that the grouchy woman below had got wind of my multitude of mice and filed a complaint.

I called out irritably, "Well, Officer, why don't you walk right in, just as every other Tom, Dick, and Harry does? The screen is unlocked."

Frowning and hesitant, he walked in. He lacked

the height and bulk of most policeman; indeed, he seemed undersized and slender. He had a dark face, high cheek-boned, and looked at me with shiny black eyes as he rebuked me in Spanish-accented English. "You should not leave your door open so—as you say—every Tom, Dick, and Harry can come in. It's asking for trouble."

"If that's what you're here to warn me about," I said curtly, "you have done your duty and may go."

He remained. His eyes went past me to the casement windows before which I stood stiffly, trying to spread myself out to conceal the cage at either end of the sill. He said, "Umm. Mice?"

I could not deny it. I kept silent—waiting.

"Please," he said, "I would like a closer look." I stepped aside.

As he crossed the room, I thought, He walks more like a Spanish matador than an officer of the law. Many Puerto Ricans, I knew, had moved into the shabby side streets on the fringes of Gramercy Park, and doubtless a Puerto Rican policeman had been assigned as suitable to the section.

He looked closely at Michael and Judith in their separate cages, then motioned toward the carton nursery. "How many little mice in there?"

"Nine," I replied briefly.

"Please, when will they come out?"

I lifted my shoulders. I was now dismally certain that when they did, it would not be into the gaiety of my planned coming-out party.

The police officer spoke in a dreamy tone. "When

I was a boy, I wanted pet mice. But my mother she cried, 'Santa Maria Purisima! Mice! No, no!' " He smiled in a superior male fashion. "Women! They fear such small creatures." He looked at me admiringly. "But not you, eh?"

"I find mice good companions," I admitted, and I felt a warm and pleasant feeling flowing between this Puerto Rican and me. I sighed. "I presume you are here to warn me that in harboring mice I am breaking the law."

His black eyes studied me. "So! That is why you looked so scared when a police officer is at your door to ask you, please, to buy tickets to the Policemen's Benefit Dance. I said to myself, 'Officer Luquillo, what is this so dignified and handsome señora guilty of?' " He smiled and his teeth shone white in his dark face. "Now I find she is guilty of mice. Well, Officer Luquillo will not report an unsanitary condition to the Health Department, so you may keep your good little companions." Then he became businesslike. "How many benefit tickets you buy, eh?"

I bought six, though I could ill afford them. As he pocketed his blackmail money, he told me his precinct number and added with a smile, "You phone me when the little mice come out, and I'll bring my boy Juan to see them. "My boy—he just crazy about mice."

I listened until I heard the elevator door close behind him; then, unbelievingly, I began to review my situation: I now had established relation with the police and the Puerto Ricans. Moreover, I admitted, facing up to my shocking behavior, I had bribed an officer not to report my mice. And anybody with an ounce of sense knows that once a person has yielded to extortion, there's usually no end to it. Other bribes are demanded. Thus the imminent coming out of nine more mice would be not the more the merrier but the more the worries and dire possibilities.

I sank into a chair and held my whirling head.

twelve

The imminent coming out of the little mice brought to my mind, one day, another possibility, even more ominous than blackmail. There might be more of a coming out than I was prepared to cope with—a coming out not only from the nursery carton but from between the bars of the cage. With growing alarm, I visualized myriads of tiny mice scurrying hither and yon in my apartment, escaping through the crack under my door and into the corridor, to scatter all through the building. I imagined the screams of the grouchy woman below.

Then, with horror, I remembered that this was the day for the monthly visit of the exterminator.

Posthaste I hied over to Third Avenue and into a hardware store to hold earnest conversation with a sympathetic clerk. I purchased what he advised and hurried home with a roll of copper screening under my arm. The rest of the day I spent with pliers in hand and bobby pins in mouth, fastening the screening over the top of the home cage and around its four sides. It took a deal of planning, contriving, and re-doing, muttering and repairing, before I succeeded in arranging the screen so that the gate could be lifted and closed again.

My precautions were perfectly timed. "I'm now attuned to mice," I congratulated myself the next morning, "and have become intuitive about their instincts and behavior," for one small, venturesome mouse had emerged from the carton to take his first look at the world. "He's the enterprising one," I thought, "the mouse most likely to succeed. He has get-up-and-get." He was golden tan and—so I deduced—the eldest son.

Impulsively I started to the phone to alert Father Lane about the mice exodus. Then I paused and glanced at the clock. He might be about to go up to the altar. Mice and Mass would not go well together. Cautiously I tiptoed back to the window sill, where, among my plants, I now kept the home cage. Michael's bachelor quarters had been banished to the less desirable location on the coffee table. I stood at a discreet distance from the window and watched.

Soon another small mouse emerged. This one was black. It took one hesitant step forward and two quick ones back. "She's the cautious one," I decided, "the mouse who will be safe, dull, and good—the daughter who will remain at home to look after her old mother." The mother was obviously uneasy now as her children ventured forth. Firmly she shooed them both back into the nursery. The tan one immediately darted out again. Mother mouse rounded him up. It took some doing, but she finally got him back inside.

Just then I had a memory of my own mother long before, when my eldest brother had been set on leaving home and making his own way in the world. My mother had clung to him, pulling him forcibly back into the house and sobbing, "When the first child leaves the home, the others will soon follow and I'll be left all alone."

Judith now showed the same instinct to keep her children under her own jurisdiction and protection. I watched her intently. As soon as she had her eldest son inside the carton, she hastily pulled up the cotton to block the exit. Then, frantically, she worked with nose and paws to push up the deodorant sand into a barrier across the opening of the carton.

Not satisfied with this double measure of security, she ran around and around the cardboard box, casing the situation before deciding on a course of action. Then she shoved at one side of the boxful of heavy mice, pushing it slowly along until its open end was against the wall of the cage. She then eased it back enough to leave a very narrow space between carton and wall—a sort of corridor. She had neatly arranged things so that there was only one path from the nursery into the world, and she was in control of it. At lane's end, she took up guard duty. She was still there when I went to bed that night.

However, the next morning—a Saturday—when I looked into the cage, I saw that she was accepting the inevitable—yielding to the right of her children to grow up and making the best of it. It had taken the mother mouse only twenty-four hours. I have known human mothers who have never achieved it.

Judith, looking matronly and indulgent, watched her toddlers emerge, one after another—six black ones and three of golden tan. They all ran about curiously inspecting their world. Under her supervision, they investigated raw oatmeal, sunflower seeds, and a container of milk. But they were familiar with a better container that had faucets, and they scrambled upon her. Apparently she was not in the mood, and, shaking them off, she jumped upon the wheel to show them how to get their exercise in captivity. Soon the nine tiny mice were all over the revolving wheel, clinging to its spokes, to their mother, to each other's tails. It was an enchanting sight—and I remembered my neighbors.

In my frayed bathrobe and hair rollers—for who cared?—I ran along the corridor to pound upon the Blackburns' door, yelling ungrammatically, "It's me! It's me! Oh, come quickly! They've come out!"

Back I ran, followed by Mrs. Blackburn in house-coat and curlers, the new baby in her arms, and close behind came Sandy and Peggy in bare feet and their towering crew-cut father fastening his trouser belt. They all crowded into my apartment in the greatest excitement and tumult.

As they gathered around the home cage, I ran to the phone, dialled, and after a moment cried into the mouthpiece, "Oh, Father Lane, they've come out! They're all over the wheel, whirling around and around as Judith turns it for them. Sometimes they're upside down—they tumble off—scramble on again—they cling to the spokes or to their mother or to each other's tails. It's hilarious! Can you hear the people shouting and the children laughing? Do come right away."

"I wish I could," he replied longingly, "but I'm scheduled to say a funeral Mass and afterward to go to the cemetery."

"A funeral Mass," I echoed. "The cemetery." I was appalled. "Oh, Father Lane, I'm so sorry I bothered you."

"Don't be," he said quickly, "for it has done me good to be reminded that there is new life running on the wheel and children shouting with laughter. Congratulate Michael for me. By the way, where is he?"

"In his bachelor quarters on the coffee table."

"Poor, lonely Michael," he said, with an audible sigh. And I felt a rush of tenderness toward the whole world because a priest who was about to perform a solemn High Mass could still be concerned for his mouse. He was saying, "Perhaps I can arrange to come and bring the altar boys this evening."

"Do," I urged. "I'll postpone the formal coming-out party until you are here."

But it could not be postponed; things simply got out of hand. The glad news spread through the building, charging the atmosphere with an electric excitement and a sort of absurd joyousness. The shouts and laughter in my apartment went out through the screen door and down the back stairs to the floor below, and reached Gentle Julia, who had just opened her door to pick up the morning paper. Clad in her bathrobe, she came puffing up and into my living room to join Mrs. Blackburn and me.

Gentle Julia, in rapture, cried above the din, "Oh, life! Oh, love! Oh, mice and men!" Then, across the cage, she said to me, "As I came up, I met Mr. Gardiner going down to walk his dog. I told him all this noise probably meant that your little mice had come out."

Fervently I hoped that the racket would not reach the grouchy woman below. Gentle Julia was calling above the noise to me, "Mr. Gardiner said that when he returns from walking Trudy, he'll bring her up to join the mouse party."

When he came, carrying his small brown mongrel, Officer Luquillo was with him. "The uproar came right through your open windows down to Twenty-second Street, where I was walking my dog," Mr. Gardiner explained. "This officer asked me, 'What's disturbing the peace?' And I told him, 'Mice.'"

"Sí, Señora," Officer Luquillo said, his smile flashing brightly. "So I came—" The remainder was drowned out by the crying of the baby, the barking of the dog, the laughter of Gentle Julia and the Blackburn parents, and the shouts of the children.

The phone rang, and the minute I put the receiver to my ear, Gladys's voice demanded, "I say! What's all the hullabaloo? Oh, I know! By Jove, they've come out. The show's on. I'll be there as fast as a taxi can take me. I'll bring my bird and refreshments."

She arrived with her parakeet in a cage, lollipops, confetti, and ice cream. Gentle Julia gave this provender a withering glance. "Entirely unsuitable for men," she pronounced, and left to return shortly with something she deemed more appropriate for men—and herself. In her wake came her cat and the blond twins. And during the ensuing festivities I had no doubt whatsoever but that I had rejoined the human race—or, to be more exact, that the human race had rejoined me.

But such unacceptable members of it!

My fastidious eyes went over them: Mr. Gardiner, holding his dog and cackling his falsetto laugh; Gentle Julia with her hair dyed to match her cat; Gladys, with her Cleopatra makeup, theatrical gestures and parakeet; Officer Luquillo, the Puerto Rican; the easy-going Blackburn parents and their noisy, undisciplined adopted children; and the gum-chewing bleached twins.

A revulsion of feeling went through me. My head ached. I longed for my pre-mice era. Furtively I glanced at the clock. It was well past the time when the mice usually hid away to sleep, yet Judith and her young remained out, running on their wheel, as if they were enjoying the hilarity they caused.

They're exhibitionists, I thought peevishly. I glanced at Michael's bachelor quarters. He had crept away to sleep, but no one missed him. Finally, Judith and her progeny retired and the people began to straggle out. Officer Luquillo lingered to say in a low tone of conspiracy, "I'll tell my boy Juan to come tonight to see the little mice. *He* won't tell anyone you have mice. O.K.?"

"O.K.," I replied wearily, and was left alone to survey the confetti-strewn floor, empty bottles, ice-cream containers, leftover lollipops, and sleeping mice. My home looks like a carnival lot on the day after, I thought, and then began to clean up the place.

That evening Father Lane arrived with a swarm of lads, and if they *were* altar boys, they were disguised as Boy Scouts. Juan, the Puerto Rican lad, was already at the window, in an attire of stretch pants and a bright open-necked shirt. The Boy Scouts, who were of various-hued skins, joined him, and one and all shouted boisterously at the antics of Judith and her toddlers on the wheel.

But not Father Lane. He laid his clerical hat on my desk and sprinted to the coffee table; then he brought the bachelor cage to the window sill, and without so much as a "May I?" to me he let Michael out. That dapper mouse streaked past my plants and over to the home cage. He ran around and around it and up over its top, stopping now and again to peer through the protective screen at the astonishing revelry that met his bright little eyes.

"He wants in," said Juan. "He wants fun, too."

Father Lane spoke to the boy in Spanish, which surprised me, for I had not known that he could. Juan's dark face brightened like a jack-o'-lantern when a candle is lit inside. He replied in a rush of voluble sounds.

Father Lane turned to me. "I asked how he happens to be your guest here, and"—his eyes crinkled—"he asked me how it happens that a grown woman like you has mice pets."

"And how, may I ask, did you explain it?"

"I said that you have mice by the grace of God," Father replied serenely.

Juan cried, "Oh, look at the father mouse!"

Michael was trying his utmost to enter the home cage to join the festivities. He gnawed at the screen; he rattled it imperiously. The toddlers came curiously to the cage side to inspect the would-be interloper. One Boy Scout observed, "If they know their father, they don't act like it."

"That's for sure," agreed another one. "His own kids are giving him the brushoff."

"But Michael—he don't like his kids, either," commented Juan disapprovingly.

"Even if he dislikes them," Father Lane said, sending a sidelong glance at me, "surely now they are too big for Michael to harm."

"Especially since I have no intention of admitting him to where he can get at them," I said dryly.

Judith ignored Michael and his frantic efforts to join her. She finished her exercise on the wheel, hopped off, and at a leisurely pace went toward the excited Michael. Then, calmly, she seemingly conversed with him through the screen.

"If she is inquiring where he has been all this time," Father Lane said sadly, "she acts as if she doesn't much care. Indeed, she seems put out at his reappearance."

"Obviously she is bored with him," I replied as she returned to the wheel. The little ones joined her, and merrily, merrily they ran, for they had learned the knack of it. We watched the mice whirling for a time, then Father Lane said in a musing voice, "I can almost sympathize with Michael's former drastic action in ridding himself of such unbeatable competition for Judith's attention."

"I'll remove him from temptation," I said and grabbed Michael's tail and plucked him with difficulty from the screen where he clung. "Come, sir, it's back into solitary for you." I swung him into the small cage, closed it, and returned it to the coffee table.

"Poor, lonely Michael," a Boy Scout said.

"Sí, poor, lonely Michael," the Puerto Rican echoed.

"Amen," said Father Lane.

I spoke with acerbity. "Father, if you are so sorry for Michael, why don't you take him back with you to the rectory?"

"Oh, I can't, not yet," he replied quickly. "I'm the chaplain of this troop of Boy Scouts and I'm scheduled to conduct a Retreat for them." He picked up his hat.

So, I thought cynically, the Boy Scout retreat allows him to retreat from his responsibilities to Michael. I set my jaw, for I meant to get rid of the male mouse.

I thought of bribes. I went to fetch the leftover lollipops. I distributed them, not overlooking Father Lane, for I knew he had a sweet tooth. Then I said, "Now you boys may draw lots to see which one gets this extraordinary mouse for his very own pet."

The Boy Scouts, one after another, shook their heads, and then one lad spoke for all: "We can't—on account of our mothers don't dig mice."

I looked at Juan. His dark eyes were full of longing but he, too, shook his head. "I can't, because my mother—she don't dig mice either," he said, proud to use the American slang term. He added, "My mother —she scream, 'Mice! Santa Maria! No! No!'"

Father Lane removed a red lollipop from his mouth to say, "Well, boys, we better be going for Mrs. Wood has had a full day and no doubt needs sleep."

And Father Lane led his Boy Scout troop out, looking back at me with a twinkle in his eye.

thirteen

One would naturally suppose that the coming-out party had somewhat accustomed the little rodents to the presence of human beings. But, no.

On the following mornings, at my unexpected appearance beside the cage there was a wild skittering of frightened mice back into the nursery. They remained hidden in the carton while I shut its entrance; when I lifted it out of the cage and placed it on the table, they stayed inside, truly as still as mice, while I cleaned the cage and Judith ran about on the table.

This frightened scamper into the carton every morning greatly facilitated my cleaning of the cage. But soon I became troubled. Of course, they needed time to learn that I was not Mary the Menace, yet I knew that as long as they had their place of refuge, their acceptance of me as a part of their daily lives would be delayed.

So one morning I dumped them into the cage and removed the nursery carton permanently. They scooted about in a veritable panic. It wrung my heart, for I also knew that sense of panic—of being exposed to unknown dangers. In compassion, I started to replace the nursery carton, then reconsidered. "No," I said decisively. "Even little mice must learn to adjust to their environment."

I put in a good supply of shredded tissue paper in which they could hide and sleep. I was now fairly certain that even if it became entangled in the wheel and they tumbled out helter-skelter, it would present no hazard to their lives. But the next morning I realized that the elimination of the nursery carton presented a hazard to my own life. For now it was not a mere matter of lifting out a closed carton full of little mice.

I stood by the table in consternation, looking down at the home cage. Within it Judith and her nine lively young scampered about. Now, how the dickens was I to get this cage cleaned? Did I dare to let them out with their mother to run around on the table?

I decided to chance it; I could think of nothing else to do. Perhaps the sensible, capable Judith could manage so that no dire consequences would follow. I opened the cage. Judith hopped out, but only one of her progeny had the temerity to hop out after her.

"It's that eldest son again," I said aloud. "The venturesome one—the mouse most likely to succeed." I waited for the others to follow. They did not—they would not. I grew impatient and, picking up the cage, unceremoniously dumped them onto the table.

They ran hurry-scurry, then finally reached their mother, who, dependable mouse that she was, solved their problem. With her nose, she lifted a newspaper edge and the tiny mice ran beneath it. The papers quivered with their movements; then, gradually, one after another peeked out and ventured forth. Soon all nine of them were busily running around, inspecting their new and larger world.

If I was one of the sights—and surely they saw me—they now accepted me as Mary the Ministrant to Mice. But I took no chances, and moved very slowly as I carried the cage into the bathroom.

When I tiptoed out again, I was extremely glad that they did not flee at the sight of me. Cautiously I approached the table and placed the cage on it, careful to make no sudden movement. Judith hopped in and nonchalantly began her exercise. Then I waited, expecting the little mice to hop in and join her on the wheel. They didn't. Time passed, and I glanced anxiously at the clock.

"You silly little pests!" I said irritably. "I can't

wait all day for you." And I made a wide, sweeping gesture to shoo them into the cage.

In an instant, there were nine wild darting streaks of black and tan in nine different directions. One flashed right off the table. I heard a small thump as it hit the floor. Hastily I glanced down but saw no mouse. Oh, great grief! What if the others followed!

Then the little mice and I lost all our self-control.

I, with a speed heretofore unprecedented even in my pre-arthritic years, sprinted around the table trying to grab the tails of small mice that were like bits of quicksilver. When I succeeded in catching one by the tail and had swung the scamp into the cage, it usually passed one or two darting out again. I needed as many arms and hands as a Hindu goddess, all swinging in different directions—north, east, south and west. Judith was no help to me at all. She trotted upon the wheel and left the whole job to me. Ultimately I did get them all into the cage, and then sank down to catch my breath.

At once, I thought of the vanished mouse.

But perhaps I had been mistaken in thinking it had fallen off the table. I devoutly hoped so. I checked those in the cage. One, two, three—up to eight. I checked and rechecked. No error. Beyond a doubt, one was missing—a tan one. Now, where has that infernal little truant scooted off to? I thought angrily.

I went down on my creaking knees and peered under the radiator, under an armchair, under a carved chest. Not a pair of bright little pinpoint eyes looked back at me. I sat back on my heels and imagined the tiny creature cowering in some dark shadow, its small heart pulsating wildly. Under normal conditions, a mouse heart beats five hundred times a minute—or so Mr. Blackburn had informed me. This one's heart must have been palpitating, for, of course, he was scared out of his mouse wits at finding himself lost in the big world with no mother to guide him. Yet—

Surely the missing one is the venturesome one—the eldest son—the cocky one, I thought. I'd bet my last dollar on it, and that he'd survive somehow. So calm down, I admonished the mouse and myself. Don't panic. Use your brain—and your instinct.

I used my brain to figure out that mouse instinct would lead the truant into a carton, for a carton represented home. I found one and, feeling vastly pleased with myself, placed a goodly supply of sunflower seeds and a bottle cap of milk in it. "I've become *en rapport* with mice," I murmured complacently as I put the carton of food on the floor near the radiator.

All during that day, my mind was only half on my memoirs as I tried to record a motor trip I had taken to Stratford-on-Avon, when I was young, to see Shakespeare's plays presented in his birthplace. I kept getting up from my writing, tiptoeing to the radiator, and bending down to peer into the carton. It remained bleakly empty, and as the afternoon waned, I became more and more worried.

That evening, when I looked in at the untouched food, an appalling realization struck me: the absentee was still a nursing mouse. Even if he ventured into the carton, he would not know how to eat, and he surely would starve to death unless my brain contrived some way to aid the mouse's instinct. But not until I was ready for bed did I think of a possible way of doing so.

Then I removed the screening on one side of the cage and turned it back, placed the cage on the floor near the radiator, and hoped to heaven the little vagrant would come home to the familiar container of milk—his mother. For he was still small enough to squeeze in between the bars of the cage to reach her.

Suddenly, my blood congealed at a horrendous possibility. What if—instead of one little mouse squeezing in—eight mice squeezed out!

I stood in uncertainty. To my mind came a swift vision of nine little mice frolicking about on the floor, slithering out through the crack under the door, capering merrily around in the corridor, scurrying curiously all through the building—to replenish it with mice.

Deciding to take the calculated risk, I left the screening turned back and went to bed. But I was careful to pull up the bedclothes so that nothing touched the floor, for I shuddered at the thought of little capersome mice climbing up the bedclothes and into bed with me. I had difficulty going to sleep.

Some time later, I woke with a sense of urgency, sat up abruptly in the dark, and started to put my bare feet on the floor, then thought better of it, retrieved them hastily, and switched on the light. In a split second, I caught a glimpse of a small ball of tan fur on top of the cage; then it vanished, I knew not where. Had it squeezed into the cage? Or had eight others already squeezed out?

Gingerly I picked my way across the floor to the cage. Inside—praise be!—there was a hectic squirming of mice. I tried to count tails. Though it was next to impossible, I thought I counted up to eight, and no matter how many times I recounted, there still were only eight. Returning the cage to the floor, I said irascibly, "If that little tramp hasn't the mouse sense he was born with, let him look to his own survival!"

I went back to bed, and after a long time of counting little mice squeezing out between cage bars, I eventually slept.

The next morning, when I picked up the cage and counted tails, lo! there were nine.

"Let us rejoice!" I cried gaily to Michael, in his bachelor quarters. "Your prodigal son, your first-born, has returned." For there wasn't a doubt in my mind but that the one who had so boldly leaped off the table into the big unknown world was indeed the same tan mouse who had been the first to emerge from the nursery. I sensed in him enterprise, daring, a certain recklessness—a mouse to be watched.

My relief at the safe return of the prodigal was superseded by a new anxiety. I knew I must not let the little mice out again to run about on the table while I scrubbed their cage.

What to do? In my past long life, I had solved many difficulties. Now I challenged myself. Were mice too much for me to cope with?

Cope, I would. But how?

fourteen

After some thought, I believed I knew how to cope with cleaning the cage. I brought out a deep bureau drawer and within it placed the cage and opened it, as Father Lane had once done for Michael. After Judith and her lively youngsters emerged to romp about in this yard of high walls, I took the cage into the bathroom for scrubbing.

However, when I put the clean cage back into the

drawer, I had a terrible time getting the frolicking mice back into it. They refused to return voluntarily to captivity. As fast as I could grab a fleeing tail and swing a small wriggling mouse inside, three other bits of mischief streaked out. I was out of breath and patience by the time I got them all safely back in the cage and the gate closed.

It was past noon when I got down to my memoirs.

For a week, the little mice made no attempt to escape from the drawer into a larger world. Then, one morning as I pursued fleeing tails, a tan mouse breezed right up the drawer side, intent on going a.w.o.l. I barely succeeded in intercepting him.

"It's the little scallawag again," I said.

Indeed, although the three tan toddlers were identical triplets in appearance, in manners (or the lack of them) one stood out. When they learned to drink milk from a dish, one tan mouse aggressively shoved all the others aside to get his own fill of milk first. He even shoved his mother rudely out of the way.

Another morning, as I watched the little mice munch sunflower seeds, it crossed my mind that *they* were never troubled by an awareness of less fortunate mice beings without enough to eat. They know nothing of starving mice, I thought. They always have food plentifully supplied, thanks to me.

That I had become provider for a large family of mice sometimes irked me. One disagreeable, blustery morning when a high rainy wind rattled my casement windows, I discovered there wasn't a drop of milk in my refrigerator. At first, this did not dismay me; in the food closet there was a package of powdered milk. I mixed some of it in a pitcher of water, cheerfully poured the thin blue liquid on my cereal and into my coffee, and ate and drank. But when I poured it into a bottle cap for Michael, and a dish for Judith and her brood, all mice sniffed in contempt and turned their backs on it. They wouldn't touch the stuff.

I looked out at the turbulent weather, then at Michael running indifferently on his wheel. "This crisis in food logistics leaves *you* untroubled—and why not?" I exclaimed, exasperated. "You have nothing to worry about. You don't have to provide for a large family of growing mice, even though they're your own. You leave it all to me."

But there is, I realized, something irrefutable in the trust and reliance tame animals put upon humans. And, of course, my sense of fairness told me that if I kept these creatures in a cage where they could not fend for themselves, it was up to me to fend for them. "But they don't have to be so pernickity about what they drink," I grumbled. Still complaining, I donned raincoat and galoshes, tied a cellophane hood over my head, and went out into the inclement weather.

Against high wind and driving rain, I pushed my way over to the Third Avenue supermarket. My umbrella turned inside out, and I was drenched to the marrow and hating all mice by the time I returned home. Dripping with rain and resentment, I emptied the thin blue stuff out of the bottle cap and the dish and refilled them with full rich milk. Then, still in my rain clothes, I watched Judith and Michael and their progeny thirstily lapping it up. There was, after all, I thought, something very rewarding in not having failed the trust of mice—come even heavy weather.

A morning or so later, I realized that the mice toddlers had grown too big to squeeze out between the cage bars and that the protective copper screen could safely be removed. As I was busy with pliers, it occurred to me that I had not seen Gentle Julia for days on end, and I wondered uneasily if she had again succumbed to her need for surcease from life. Well, that was her problem. Then I had a galling thought: I tended to the needs of mice, but was I becoming indifferent to human needs? To prove I was not—but complaining to myself about weak characters who escaped from hard life into hard liquor—I went downstairs with a pot of strong black coffee. Julia wasn't in very good shape—clothes unpressed and eyes swollen—but I forced her to drink plenty of coffee and then go back upstairs with me to help with the mouse chores.

We placed Michael's bachelor quarters at one end of the table and the bureau drawer full of frolicking little mice at the other. When I let Judith out to run around, bleary-eyed Gentle Julia commented disapprovingly, "Judith certainly looks stodgy and matronly."

"Yes," I said. "She reminds me of human mothers who have that same smug air of 'I have produced young, and that is all the world need expect from *me.*'"

Judith was ignoring Michael in his small cage. She

ambled about, stopped meditatively to scratch an ear, and sat up and washed her face. Gentle Julia observed, "I suppose that's her equivalent of powdering her nose."

Finally, with a bored manner, Judith went to the cage, and Michael excitedly leaped to the bars to welcome her. Frantically he tried to get to her, but she maintained her air of boredom. Gentle Julia commented compassionately, "Poor Michael is married to an older, matronly mouse. Perhaps he has a mother complex."

"There's no doubt that Judith is the mother type," I said. "Home and family are enough for her; they fill all her emotional needs."

"If her mother ever gave her the sage advice that her husband must always come first, Judith shows no inclination to heed it," said Gentle Julia.

We both watched as Judith turned a cold shoulder on Michael and returned to mother her family.

Then it was time to clean Michael's cage, and when Gentle Julia let him out, he went like a streak of lightning over to the home cage, all eagerness to squeeze in between the bars to reach his wife (and perhaps his offspring).

His children came curiously to the bars and thrust out their tiny noses to touch his, and Gentle Julia wondered aloud if he knew he was their father.

"Who knows?" I said. "Perhaps they are saying, 'Hello, Dad,' and he replies, 'Hi, there, sons and daughters!' But," I added, "if he can tell which is which, it's more than I can. They're all 'it's' to me—

with the exception of that tan one, who shows definite characteristics. He not only has Michael's jaunty air, but more daring, more audacity."

Then Michael began to run around and around the cage, prancing in his dancing-master fashion, and I remarked, "He reminds me of certain empty-headed young men who depend more on their good looks and charm than on such solid traits of character as Judith uses in life."

"Theirs is certainly a misalliance." Gentle Julia looked at Michael with pity. "He with his gay agility and emotional nature is mated to this dull domestic drudge, who will never keep pace with him—a cold mouse if ever I saw one."

"No doubt he is headed straight for a psychiatrist's couch," I said caustically, "but even so I shall not admit him into the home cage."

"Why ever not?"

"Because I've had my fill of mice, that's why," I said firmly, and, grabbing Michael by the tail, I swung him over into the bachelor quarters and slammed shut the gate. "Sublimate it, Michael," I said. "Apply reason to your love, as Dante advised."

"I think strong characters are often cruel," Gentle Julia said, in anything but a gentle tone, and I noticed her face was beginning to quiver. She set down her empty coffee cup with a clatter and strode out.

Her parting remark scratched like a burr until, to prove to myself that I was not cruel, I gave Michael an apple core to comfort him. He was not comforted, and retreated to sit awhile in a corner of his cage, looking sheepish and apologetic. Then, suddenly, he leaped upon his wheel and ran furiously, madly. Was this sublimation, I wondered?

For a time, I mused over the universal drive toward mating that keeps creation going. Then I removed the newspapers from my table and the subject of mice from my mind, and settled down again to my memoirs.

In deep absorption, I was describing a day in the nineteen-twenties when I was lunching at the Algonquin's Round Table and listening to—when suddenly I was jolted out of my past into the realization that my present was being invaded by noise, turmoil, and confusion. In through the doorway surged a boisterous crowd. Astounded, I looked about and saw children of all sizes and colors milling around me, sweeping past in waves of talk and laughter, to arrive at the window where the little mice still romped in the home cage.

As a young woman was swept past she looked at me with the utmost astonishment and stammered, "Oh, dear—er—Sandy didn't tell me this was a private home."

"It isn't," I snapped. "Not any more." And I returned to my writing.

After a time, the tide of children, laughter, and turbulence ebbed out of my home and down the corridor. I did not know then, and I still don't know, whether it was Sandy's Sunday-school class from the Marble Collegiate Church, come to view me living in brotherly love with mice, or Peggy's kindergarten out on a nature-study jaunt. But I did know that my life had become too full of mice and people.

"That does it!" I exclaimed, rising angrily. "Enough is enough!" And I went to the phone to tell Father Lane so.

I spilled over with complaints. "The popularity of my apartment has increased in ratio to the multiplicity of mice," I told him. "Why, a moment ago a personally conducted tour of sightseeing, babbling children interrupted my memoir-writing."

"Good!" Father Lane replied. "A present full of living children and mice is preferable to a past populated by ghosts. I've told you so before."

His lack of sympathy added fuel to my wrath. "Even before the children barged in," I went on indignantly, "I had to go downstairs and dose that Miss Tate with strong coffee to overcome the effects of stronger drink. Then after she came up and helped me with the mice, she left in high dudgeon, accusing me of being a cruel woman. And I still have to tend those mice—"

"You magnify your troubles," Father Lane said shortly.

"I'd like to see you minimize eleven mice, nine still growing," I snapped, and he replied in like manner, "I fail to see why you blame me for your troubles."

"Because your Michael is responsible for them— that's why," I cried angrily.

There followed a short silence in which I regretted having acted so humanly toward a priest, and in which he evidently regretted his own behavior. For when he spoke again it was in his grave tone. "I suggest a solution to your problems." For an awful moment, I thought he meant prayer, but he continued cheerily, "Take Judith and her little ones up to Central Park and turn them loose into the springtime."

I noted sourly that he had not included Michael in this springtime excursion, but I did not mention his oversight. I merely said icily, "Cage pets are not equal to dealing with life in the raw," and ended, with a martyr's sigh, "I suppose I shall have to keep them."

However, as it turned out, I couldn't keep them. For the very next day my landlord came to see me and got right to the point. "I've received a complaint about your mice. They go or you do. You can't raise rodents on these premises." And he made his exit.

At first, I thought I'd have to make a clean sweep; then I reflected that he had said 'raising' mice must stop. I could surely retain one mouse. I decided to risk it. Because, I assured myself, I have to keep Michael until Father Lane comes and gets him. As for Judith and her progeny—I must get rid of them. And although I had complained bitterly to Father Lane of the nuisance of sharing life with mice, I felt sad as I prepared to take the mother mouse and toddlers to a pet shop. A series of maneuvers enabled me to transfer Michael into the home cage and Judith and her young into his smaller one. It was crowded, but it would do for the trip.

I placed the small cage in a shopping bag and put on my hat. Then I paused, for I was loath to arrive at the pet shop—and I a gray-haired woman—with mice pets. Perhaps I could pretend I was a kindergarten teacher disposing of the children's mice. But this out-and-out deception was too much for my conscience. Acting on inspiration, I invited Peggy, who was home from school, to accompany the mice and me. I would trust to the proprietor's powers of deduction.

He was not an old man, but he dragged one foot and his face was twisted sidewise by a stroke. As I took the cage out of my shopping bag, I glanced at Peggy. "I have assured her you will provide a good home for these mice," I said.

Above the screams of parrots, the chattering of monkeys, and the barking of dogs, he replied loudly, "I sure will, and the mice'll have plenty of company here."

Peggy said gloomily, "But Michael is going to be awful lonesome at home all alone on the window sill."

On impulse, I inquired of the proprietor, "Would two males get along well in one cage?"

"If there's no female to make trouble," he replied, "they will."

I told him to pick out a boy mouse for Peggy to take back home. On second thought, I added, "Select one of the tan ones if it's a male." One was, the proprietor assured me, and returned him to the cage, which I replaced in the shopping bag.

On the way home, Peggy named the boy mouse

Sandy, after her brother. She skipped along beside me, singsonging, "Michael's going to be glad—glad to get his son back. Michael's going to get a surprise—a surprise. Yippee!"

When I put Sandy into the home cage, Michael was glad—glad, all right. But it was I who got the surprise.

fifteen

When I put Sandy into the big cage he hotfooted it to Michael, but his father did not recognize Sandy either as his son or as a young mouse in need of acceptance.

Michael attacked him tooth and nail.

Sandy, terrified, ran up to the top of the cage and clung there. And I, full of sympathy for this teen-age mouse in his first experience with rejection and hostility, looked with extreme disapproval upon Michael. I was shocked at this display of enmity and refusal to share.

Michael must have become a maladjusted mouse, I conjectured, for the pet-shop keeper had assured me that two males would get along well together if no female were present. Michael had never before known any mouse except Judith. He'd been willing enough to share with her. But since then he had lived in a closed society of one mouse, one bottle cap of milk, one portion of sunflower seeds, and one wheel, which apparently he was loath to share.

He'll soon adjust to sharing, I thought.

But he didn't.

As time passed, true, he did grudgingly allow Sandy to eat, drink and run upon the wheel. But alone. Michael wanted no togetherness. If Sandy attempted to eat, drink or run upon the wheel with Michael, the small mouse was attacked fiercely. The astonished Sandy would flee in fright up into the cage top and skulk there until Michael's anti-social behavior had somewhat abated.

Much as I frowned upon Michael's sharp unfriendliness, I disapproved equally of Sandy's behavior. It seemed to me he was not meeting the situation heroically. His timid conduct convinced me that he was not, as I had previously hoped, the daring young mouse who had been the first to emerge from the nursery, the reckless one who had streaked off my table, the bold one who had tried to go A.W.O.L. over the drawer wall. For a time, I was positive that Sandy could not possibly be the devil-may-care eldest son.

But as the days passed and Sandy grew bigger, he no longer fled in fear. He would whirl, stand up on his hind legs and extend his claws, keeping Michael at his distance. I sensed in Sandy a mounting hatred, not only for Michael but for all the world's evils. It seemed to me that Sandy was assuming a moral attitude, condemning Michael as a heinous sinner.

Once, I told him, "Sandy, Michael's behavior pattern has been set awry by a solitary life in which his ability to communicate with other mice has been damaged. It has nothing to do with sin or virtue, you can take my word for it." But, needless to say, nothing I told him made any difference, and in that minature animal kingdom the situation remained in status quo for a time.

Then, one morning when I was feeding the two mice, it occurred to me that Sandy had grown to Michael's size. By the next morning, the same realization must have dawned on Sandy, for as I was having my coffee, I became aware of a terrific disturbance in the cage. Of late, when I had heard such battle skirmishes, I had looked the other way, for I was fed up with the occasional regrettable goings-on in the cage. But this one was assuming the proportions of a full-scale war and sounded so deadly that I became uneasy. I looked.

Within a dust cloud of sunflower seeds and sand, there whirled two small furious bodies. It was a fight —a real fight. I rushed to the window sill, opened the cage gate, and whammed the two small combatants with a pencil until they separated. One promptly took to his heels and fled through the gate to hide among my plants. Quickly I slammed down the gate and hooked it.

When I had sufficient command of my emotions to investigate, I saw to my astonishment that it was now not Sandy who had turned tail and run; it was Michael. And I felt a vague scorn when I saw that erstwhile jaunty tan mouse cowering at the far end of the window sill. One eye was closed. The end of his tail was missing. He was minus tufts of fur, and his bared skin was torn and bleeding. I felt called upon to make excuses for him. "You had the sense to flee from imminent death, Michael," I said encouragingly. And as he nursed his wounds, I forgot his wrongdoings, and, full of pity, I put salve on him. Then I brought out the small wire-mesh box I had long ago put away. I layered it with soft cotton and tenderly placed the mauled mouse upon it.

With apprehension, I now turned my attention to the other small warrior, expecting to find young Sandy mutilated. He didn't have a mark on him. Not one. He ran merrily, merrily upon the wheel.

"So it *is* you," I said. "The daring young mouse, the bold one. You were biding your time, eh? You were waiting until you were big enough to lick your own father, throw him out of his home, and take possession of his wheel." And it certainly roused my ire to see that cheeky teen-ager enjoying the spoils of his victory. I forgot that Good had triumphed over Evil, that Sandy had fought only to gain his rightful place in the sun.

Muttering disapproval of Sandy, I dispossessed him

of the wheel and cage, and as he frisked about on the window sill, I restored Michael into his own spacious domicile. But he did not run upon his wheel. He just wasn't up to it; he was done in. Disconsolately he crawled into the cotton I placed near him. Then I put Sandy into the prison cell of the small wire box.

That evening, when the mice emerged in their separate abodes, Michael still looked battle-fatigued, but he made a feeble effort to take his exercise on the wheel. I let Sandy out of his cramped quarters to take his exercise on the window sill. But first he had some unfinished business to attend to. He made an enraged dash straight for the big cage and tried to get in at his father.

Michael, ready to forgive and forget, came amiably to the cage bars and stuck out his nose. Sandy bit it viciously. Michael hastily withdrew, and now it was he who looked rejected. Sandy backed up and climbed onto a flowerpot, took a stance as if measuring the distance, and made a furious leap at the cage, trying by sheer force of propulsion to inject himself between the cage bars. It was no go. He returned to the flowerpot and was all set to have a second try when I grabbed his tail and threw him, wriggling furiously, back into the prison cell.

Sandy, infuriated, tried to gnaw away the wire mesh of the box. Is this tempestuous adolescent mouse, I asked myself, bent upon more revenge? Is he motivated by pure cussedness? Well, I decided, he will probably cool off by tomorrow and forget today's events, for a mouse cannot possibly remember, let alone hold a grudge, for twenty-four hours. I went to bed feeling certain that in the morning I could return Sandy to the big cage with safety.

But the minute I did—what a fight! It took a ruler now to wham them apart. I grabbed Sandy's tail, yanked him out, and dropped him where he landed, then anxiously turned my attention to Michael. In a corner of the cage, he nursed fresh wounds.

And Sandy? That young ruffian was pacing up and down the window sill, as if only waiting until my back was turned to make a final assault upon his father and finish him off. Watching him, I was astounded that such a small creature could contain so much rage. I questioned again, Was that rage directed against the parent who had rejected him or against the general lack of brotherly love in the world?

Who knows? I pondered. But if Sandy were a human, his religion would be of the stark, punishing, unforgiving variety. Perhaps he'd be a Calvinist, and had he lived in past ages, he would have had Michael burned at the stake. I sighed. Whatever Sandy's motivation, it was evident he had had his fill of Michael and his shenanigans and was seething with an unquenchable hatred toward Michael that could be wiped out only by his blood and death. I knew I had to get rid of one or the other of them. There was no question which one, for Michael belonged to Father Lane, who soon, I devoutly hoped, would reclaim his mouse.

"Because I, too, am fed up with your hostility and

mean refusal to share life and being with others," I told Michael with severity.

As for Sandy, all day long I considered various possible fates for him. The pet shop would not do, for although it was possible that Sandy hated only Michael, who had rejected him, on the other hand this might have caused Sandy to hate, reject, and fight the whole world. He was definitely not a mouse to be sold to kindergartens. I tapped my chin and pondered. The thought of Gentle Julia's gaunt cat, Cassius, passed through my mind. But no, valiant Sandy deserved a better destiny. I thought of chloroform and hastily dismissed it, too.

Sandy is a fighter. He deserves a chance to fight for survival and to make a life for himself, I mused. He was daring, boldness, ingenuity. Surely he has demonstrated that he can take care of himself. He was, in fact, the very mouse most suited to carry out Father Lane's idea.

"Yes," I said decisively, "I shall turn Sandy loose in the springtime in Central Park."

sixteen

I gave Sandy what preparation I could for going out into the world on his own. From a closet, I fetched a blue pasteboard box marked "Tiffany" in which glassware had been delivered; I poked air holes in it and put in shredded tissue paper, sunflower seeds, and milk. Then I removed Michael's cage from the window sill to the safe distance of the coffee table and let Sandy out of his wire-box prison, so that during the night he could run about among the plants and go in and out of the Tiffany box and become accustomed to it.

The next morning, I saw with satisfaction that Sandy chose his new dwelling to retire in for the day's sleep. Michael's cage I replaced on the sill, for he, too, slept. Peace reigned all day, and I began to have qualms about letting a small mouse loose in big Central Park.

However, when Sandy emerged that evening onto the sill and perceived that Michael was again in the territory, his combustible temper flared. He was certainly a mouse of quick reflexes. He streaked over to the big cage and again attempted to get in at his father. Debonair Michael came promptly to the bars ready to demonstrate his forgiveness and undying affection. Sandy clawed him, and Michael, with a squeak of surprise and pain, fled. When I snatched Sandy by the tail, he twisted about violently, trying to nip my fingers. I flung him into the wire box and locked it; any lingering reluctance to get rid of him had now left me.

The next day was Saturday, and in the late afternoon I made some final preparations, for I meant to dispose of Sandy on my way to confession. First I cleaned and replenished the blue Tiffany box. Then I put in generous portions of sunflower seeds and oatmeal as I said encouragingly to Sandy, "I'm packing a nice lunchbox for you. You're going on a lovely picnic up in Central Park."

He had been furiously gnawing the wire mesh,

trying to get out of the box, yet when I opened it and tried to entice him into Tiffany's, he clung to the walls of his prison cell and refused to budge.

"Oh, come, now, Sandy," I coaxed. "You're going to have all the big outdoors in springtime to run about in."

Mulishly he chose to stay where he was. Finally exasperated, I was about to grab his tail, but thought better of it and shook him vigorously from the wire box into Tiffany's. After I had closed it and tied it with a yellow ribbon, I sighed in relief.

In the evening, I started earlier than usual for church and got off the bus at Sixty-fourth Street. I could feel Sandy thumping energetically about in the box as I entered Central Park at the Zoo, the vicinity I had selected as the place where Sandy was most likely to succeed.

As I hurried anxiously through the gloaming, I noted that most of the wild animals had retired into the inner cages of the buildings and only a few people loitered in the evening hush. I walked primly by an idle ice-cream vender and a listless balloon man, both of whom eyed me—I thought—with suspicion. Uneasily I wondered if it was against the law to abandon a mouse in the Park.

With quick steps, I went past the cafeteria terrace, where the big umbrellas were folded for the night like enormous morning-glories. I hurried past the rear courtyard, now quiet, where in daytime there was the noisy hustle-bustle of trucks delivering rattling milk cans, bundles of meat, and boxes of vegetables. Not only would food be easily available but also other mice. "So you'll find yourself a nice girl friend, Sandy," I encouraged him. "And there's no better place to spoon in than the Park under a full moon."

We reached an uphill winding path that led under shadowy evening-still trees. Here all seemed deserted. Furtively I glanced about in the violet twilight to make certain I was unobserved. Then I set down the Tiffany box under the overhanging branches of a honeysuckle bush and lifted the lid.

Instantly, Sandy's tiny tan head popped up, and he looked about in great wonder as if to say, "My, oh, my! How tall the plants on the window sill have grown!" I craned my neck to look upward at the lofty treetops, and thought how very, very tall they must look to a mouse!

A sparrow hopped by, twittering. Sandy stared at it. Why, I thought, he has never before seen any animals except mice and me. "That sparrow is nothing— nothing at all, Sandy," I told him. "Just you wait till you see pigeons—and squirrels." I was about to mention lions, bears, and elephants, but reconsidered. "You're going to have a high old time in the Park, little fellow. Well—goodbye, Sandy, and good luck."

But I made the mistake of looking back. Sandy still peered about in wonder. He looked very small. I stopped, irresolute. Then I remembered who keeps His eye on sparrows—and even smaller things. "I commend Your little creature into Your care," I murmured.

Then I walked away, around the empty, silent cafeteria, and again entered the Zoo, where I saw that a lion was now in his outer cage and was stalking up and down, lashing his tail. And I felt it incumbent upon me to warn him. "Look to yourself," I said, "for a mouse is in the streets."

When finally I arrived in the basement chapel and creaked down on my stiff-jointed knees within the shadowy confessional, I hurried through the opening ritual, then whispered to Father Lane of the deed I had perpetrated in the Park.

"You've no need to worry about Sandy's safety," he comforted me. "Soon Sandy will be mayor of all the mice along Fifth Avenue."

"It's not Sandy I'm worried about," I whispered. "It's the lions, the tigers and the elephants."

Father chuckled, for he had been told of Michael and Sandy's combats. Then he spoke softly, as priests do in the confessional. "That little fellow really is a fighter, isn't he? Let us hope he continues to fight for equal rights in the world. Well, and how is Michael?"

"His surface wounds are healing," I reported, "and in time the fur will grow over his scars, but the once-long scroll of his tail will henceforth always come to an abrupt end." After a pause I added firmly, "Father, in my opinion Michael is a well-chastened mouse, quite ready to return to the church."

Father Lane reflectively rubbed his nose. "There's nothing I'd like better than to have Michael with me again," he said, "but unfortunately I must give a series of radio talks on 'the Catholic Hour,' so as a special favor to me, could you keep him a while longer?"

"No, Father, I can't," I said bluntly. "For I doubt I can forget and forgive Michael's mean hostility to another mouse—his own son, at that."

"Now, now, you must forgive others as you exp—" Father began severely, then realized he was speaking of mice, and added testily, "Well, if you won't share your life with Michael, please find a good home for him."

But that was not easy. When I offered him to Sandy and Peggy, they were ecstatic, but their mother was not. Why should she be? I acknowledged. As matters stand, her children have all the fun and I have all the work of caring for the mouse.

When I offered Michael to Gladys, she cried, "I say! Clean a mouse cage every day as well as a bird cage? Do you think me balmy?"

And obviously Gentle Julia could not keep a mouse with her cat—not for long.

There seemed no haven for Michael except the pet shop.

So one sunny day Peggy and Sandy and I set off. As we walked along Third Avenue, the children lagged, glum and silent, and I was left to my own thoughts while I carried the shopping bag that contained Michael in his cage. How many vicissitudes this mouse has survived, I mused, by refusing to accept defeat. He had become a personality—achieved a name for himself, hyphenated—Monk-Mouse. He had had his share in forming events, not world-shaking ones but important enough to assure that in the future things would not be as they had been before he had passed by. Could we all say as much? True, he had not established a good relationship with his son, but he had entered into relation with beings many times his own size—children, a priest, an elderly woman. Now it seemed a pity that he should become once more only an anonymous mouse.

My steps lagged, too; we were nearing the pet shop.

When we entered the clamor and odor of the shop, the proprietor with the dragging foot remembered me. He asked humorously, "More mice?"

"One," I replied shortly, bringing forth Michael in his cage. The proprietor took one look. "She's pregnant!"

"*He* is fat," I corrected starchily. In recent weeks, he had indeed put on weight.

The proprietor took Michael from his cage and examined him carefully as Peggy tugged at my skirt and pointed. When I looked, I saw a thin gray cat stalking us, licking his chops. The proprietor's glance went covertly from fat mouse to thin cat, and in horror I thought, Is *that* to be the final destination of a mouse of distinction?

The proprietor said tentatively, "The cage?"

"The children want it back to play with," I said.

"Then I'll put the mouse into this," and from the sawdust-strewn floor he picked up a crumpled paper sack. He was thrusting Michael inside—

"Stop!" I cried, in a ringing voice. "This mouse

has made a name for himself—a hyphenated name—
and he has sojourned with a Jesuit in a Park Avenue
rectory. He is not going into a paper sack!"

Whereupon I snatched Michael from the astonished proprietor, put him into his cage and the cage
into my shopping bag, and said, "Come, children."

As they followed with alacrity, I heard the man behind us exclaim, "Wow! What a character!"

"So I'm a character with a mouse," I said haughtily
over my shoulder, and Sandy yelled back, "D'ya
wanna make something of it?" Peggy looked back and
stuck out her tongue. Rude, but endearing.

We walked on the double back up Third Avenue,
bouncy as a funeral band playing lively music as it
returns from the cemetery. The children skipped
along, singsonging again. "Mrs. Wood's going to keep
Michael. Mrs. Wood's going to keep Michael—"

"Oh, shut up," I snapped.

"O.K.," they said, grinning happily up at me.

Upon arriving at my apartment, I slammed the
cage onto the window sill with such a bang that it
knocked Michael off his wheel. I said angrily, "So I'm
stuck with this mouse until either one or the other
of us departs this life."

The children, jumped up and down with joy.
"Whoopee!" shouted Sandy. "Yippee!" yelled Peggy.

seventeen

On a warm humid evening in late summer, I was sitting before the wide-open casements in my rocking chair, reading Martin Buber's *I and Thou,* when an unexpected "Ahem" sounded outside my screen door. Glancing over my shoulder, I saw Father Lane outside.

I called, "The screen is unhooked. Come right in, Father." He entered, clerical hat in one hand and mopping his perspiring brow with a handkerchief in the other. "Do pardon my dropping in like this, but I was on my way to make a sick call at the Columbus Hospital and thought I'd stop in to see you."

"To see your mouse, you mean," I said.

"All right, to see my mouse."

"He's out."

"Out? What do you mean out?"

"I mean out taking his evening constitutional."

Father Lane glanced at the empty cage, then out through the open windows. He laughed. Michael was on the window ledge trotting back and forth along the outer rim, now and again pausing nonchalantly to peer down to the street far, far below.

"It makes my blood curdle," I commented. "I simply cannot endure to look down from a dizzy height. Sit down, Father. Let me take your hat."

"No, thanks, I'm late. I can only stay a moment."

He laid his hat on the sill and clucked. Immediately, Michael trotted inside and walked docilely into Father Lane's cupped hand. Enormously pleased, he exclaimed, "Why, my mouse still knows me!"

"Before a priest becomes all puffed up with sinful pride because he is recognized by a mouse," I said, "let him consider the possibility that what the mouse recognizes are the sunflower seeds concealed in the wily Jesuit's hand."

Father Lane ignored my sarcasm. "Aside from the loss of a third of his tail, Michael seems to have recovered from combat."

"From his surface wounds, yes," I agreed. "But who knows what he may suffer as a result of his unusual experiences? For surely Michael has travelled more than most mice, seen more of the world, known more people." I warmed to my subject. "He's had his ups and downs, his ups to a Park Avenue rectory and the companionship of an erudite Jesuit, his downs to a side-street apartment and the companionship of an anti-social widow of meagre intellect and means. Michael," I concluded, "has had to adjust to radically different environments and personalities."

"So he has." Father Lane's expressive face was meditative. "He has had more than his mouse share of hopes and disappointments, woes and joys."

"He has lived a celibate's life," I said musingly as I rocked. "And then he has loved, married, and propagated a family, had the sorrow of having his beloved taken from him, and known the bitterness of fathering an ungrateful son. He has sinned against that son, and—let us hope—repented. He has experienced the wretchedness of defeat, and now he knows the long-drawn-out sadness of aging in loneliness."

There followed a silence in which I watched Michael sitting up in the priest's hand munching sunflower seeds. Finally, Father Lane said, "Michael looks serenely submissive to God's will."

"He has acquiesced to life, as I have," I said softly. "The mouse knows, as I do now, that life must be lived, worked, and suffered to its very end."

"Blessed be God," said Father Lane.

"There was a time," I reflected, "when to me a mouse was only a disgusting little rodent that sent shivers up my spine. Then I was given a mouse of mine own, and for a time a mouse was a mouse was a mouse. But now"—I looked at Michael in Father Lane's hand and went on in a marvelling tone—"now forevermore when I see a mouse dart in or out of a hole, I shall pause to question, What are his individual characteristics, his personal problems, his loves, his conflicts? What are his abilities to solve, circumvent, or survive his problems? Never again," I declared, "will a mouse be only an '*it*' to me, for I shall see '*Thou*' even in a mouse."

Michael stepped sedately from Father Lane's hand onto the sill, trotted into his cage and awkwardly mounted the wheel. Father Lane remarked in disapproval, "He's become far too fat and paunchy."

"Certainly he's no longer a slim, jaunty young mouse," I admitted.

"He needs more exercise," Father Lane said.

"Observe how he takes it," I said. "Not with the onetime zest of spring. No 'over hill, over dale, through bush, through briar.' Oh, no! But rather with autumn's prudent watch-your-step-old-boy, the wisdom of middle age."

"We're all getting on," said Father Lane, running his hand through his thinning hair. "No doubt as Michael ambles along, he ruminates over the credits and debits of a long, full, rich life."

"As I do," I murmured. Then wryly I said, "I'm no longer writing my memoirs of important people and events. I'm too busy with inconsequential events and unimportant people—and a mouse."

"Only God knows what is and is not of consequence and importance," Father Lane said.

"Well, I know one thing," I said ruefully, "I must have more than my share of animal nature to have established relation with a mouse."

"Not necessarily." Father cast me a keen glance. He gestured toward the paperback in my lap. "Martin

Buber says, as nearly as I can recall, that when relation sometimes occurs between animals and people, it is usually *not* with persons of predominantly animal nature but, on the contrary, with those whose true nature is spiritual."

"That's a comfort," I said, in a dry tone. Then I added, "At any rate, I know my mouse and my mouse knows me. Please note, Father, that I said, '*my*' mouse, for I'm well aware, Father, that I'm the one who will scrub his cage every morning of my life until either Michael or I will die." I sent Father Lane an accusing glance. "Admit, Father, that you've no intention of taking on that disagreeable chore again."

Father Lane frowned. "It's not that I mind scrubbing his cage," he protested. "It's that when Michael is with me, I spend too much time playing with the little fellow, time better employed elsewhere."

"I wonder. I myself feel the wiser and richer for having known mice. In fact, I now feel tuned in to mice, men, and the universe. I realize now that no one should live alone, and like it. And so—"

Shrill voices cried in the corridor, "Aunt Mary! Aunt Mary!" For so Peggy and Sandy now called me. My screen door was yanked open; the two children burst in and sprinted to the window sill.

Their mother rushed in next, her new infant draped carelessly over one arm. She was dressed for a night on the town. Lumbering after her came Mr. Blackburn, carrying a bundle of diapers and a nursing bottle. Hastily they greeted Father Lane. Then Mrs. Blackburn said to me, "Thanks a million for minding our little monsters tonight," and unceremoniously dumped the baby into my lap as the tall father deposited the supplies on the sill.

The baby began to cry, and as the parents exited, the mother called over her shoulder, "Burp him," and Mr. Blackburn added, "We'll be back by midnight." And then they were gone.

Father Lane lifted his brows. "You haven't much privacy, have you? But isn't it hazardous, leaving your door on the latch? Anybody could come in."

"Anybody could—and does," I replied as I burped the baby, "and certainly it's hazardous. Life is. As to privacy, I've had none since my pre-mice age."

I rocked the baby's cries down to cooing, and spoke thoughtfully. "It's as if a mouse had fetched in a thread, which pulled in a string, which brought in a cord, which dragged in a rope, which hauled in a cable, upon which a bridge was built, so people could come in to me."

I gave Father a wide smile. "Build a better mouse and the whole world will beat a path to your door."

Father Lane nodded and after a moment said, "God does not always hand his work over to the angels."

Then he took Michael into his cupped hands. He lifted the mouse high, high up, in the posture I had so often seen him assume at the altar when he was the celebrant at Mass and offered up the Host to God. And now Father Lane's whole attitude and expression were as rapt and reverent as if he were presenting the mouse to the attention of heaven and offering up thanks to God for the marvel of creation as manifested in so small a creature as a mouse.